D1707006

THE
YESTERTIME
EFFECT

A Novel of Time Travel

YESTERTIME SERIES #2

Andrew Cunningham

Copyright © 2022 Andrew Cunningham
All rights reserved.
ISBN- 9798414032687

Books by Andrew Cunningham

Thrillers
Wisdom Spring
Deadly Shore

Yestertime Time Travel Series
Yestertime
The Yestertime Effect

"Lies" Mystery Series
All Lies
Fatal Lies
Vegas Lies
Secrets & Lies
Blood Lies
Buried Lies

Eden Rising Series
Eden Rising
Eden Lost
Eden's Legacy

Children's Mysteries
(as A.R. Cunningham)
The Mysterious Stranger
The Ghost Car
The Creeping Sludge
The Sky Prisoner
The Ride of Doom

To Charlotte ... for always being there...

PART ONE

Chapter 1

BOSTON, MASSACHUSETTS—2023

Hal March opened the door to his condo with care, his skin prickling from fear. Had they located him yet? Well, he would know in a second. He pushed open the door.

Silence.

That didn't mean anything. They were silent by nature, or by training. He turned on the lights. Hell, if they were in there, he may as well see them coming.

More silence.

Slowly, he checked each room and in less than a minute was convinced that he was alone. His place hadn't been ransacked either. Luck was momentarily on his side, so he had to move fast.

He raced to his closet and pulled out a suitcase and his backpack. Hal had a feeling that where he was going, he wouldn't need anything more than that. But even that might be too much.

He opened his safe in the back of the closet and pulled out the contents: $10,000 in cash, his 9mm handgun, his correspondence with Ray Burton and Natalie O'Brien, and with James Robards, as well as a lot of papers that he had a feeling would be worthless very soon. He threw the unimportant papers into his suitcase, and the gun, money, correspondence, and some clothes into his backpack. Then he went through the house and collected everything he thought he would need. It wasn't much. He'd never been on the run before, so he had no experience with this type of thing.

He looked at his watch. It took him thirty-five minutes to pack up everything necessary. What did that say about his life? He looked around his condo. Would this be the last time he would ever see it? Quite possibly. He was feeling less sentimental than he thought he would upon leaving. But then, when your ass is on the line, there is no time for sentiment.

He took the elevator down to the parking garage. He had already worked out this part of it in his head. He couldn't use his car for long. They'd be looking for it. But he felt safe driving it to the other side of the city. Like his condo, that too would then be abandoned.

When he saw on the news earlier in the day that James Robards had been murdered, Hal knew that he was next. The police called it a random act of violence. Hal knew better.

When they went through Robards' things, the NSA would find all of the correspondence between Robards and Hal about time travel. Then they would come after Hal. Everyone connected in any way with time travel would have to be eliminated. He had already seen it happen two years earlier when several people closely involved in the Time Travel Project had been murdered. It was part of what drove Ray Burton to enter the time portal. And it was what was probably going to force Hal to do the same.

He had been safe up until now. His involvement was strictly on the sidelines. The NSA knew that Ray had contacted him and that a suspected time traveler had once worked for him. But it wasn't enough for the NSA to take action against him. Until recently. Now, the NSA wasn't just going after the travelers; they were even going after those on the periphery. What had caused them to widen the scope of their targets?

The 45-minute drive through the streets of Boston from his

condo was anything but routine. Hal spent the whole time looking in his rearview mirror.

So far, so good.

His phone rang. It was Joyce, the receptionist, office manager, bookkeeper, and who knows what else of his small magazine publishing company, *Antiques, Etc.* Hal hesitated but then answered it.

"Hi, Joyce."

"Hal, what's going on?" Her voice was shaky and tinged with fear. "Where are you?"

"I'm just about home," Hal lied.

"Come back. Some government men are going through the office, looking for something. They said they are going to shut down the magazine unless you show up here."

"Tell them to pound sand. I might not see you again, Joyce, and if I don't, know that I enjoyed working with you."

He hung up. He didn't have to worry about Joyce. A year earlier, soon after he'd begun corresponding with James Robards, he'd gone to the bank with Joyce and had set up a safe-deposit box in both their names. If she had been confused by the actions, she didn't show it. Since meeting Ray Burton, strange things had been going on with Hal, and she knew better than to ask. If at any time he had to leave quickly, Joyce knew to visit the box and empty it after things had calmed down. She didn't know what was in it but suspected that it was Hal's way of taking care of her. Joyce had been with Hal at the magazine since its inception, and had been a trusted and loyal employee. Hal had made sure that there was enough money in the safe deposit box to more than make up for the fact that she would be suddenly unemployed.

He parked his car in the parking garage in Brookline that he used daily. He was only a block from his office, but the government bozos were on their way to his condo right now. Some were probably there already. He broke into a sweat as he realized how close he'd come to dying.

He locked the car and threw the keys into a nearby trash can. It wouldn't be locked long. The NSA would discover his vehicle and search it, inch by inch. He removed the sim card from his phone and crushed the phone with a piece of concrete he found in the corner of the garage. He broke the sim card in half and threw the phone and sim card pieces in different garbage cans.

He left by way of a side entrance and walked the two blocks to his usual lunch spot, an old-fashioned diner. It was three o'clock, and they were about to close for the day.

"Hey, Mr. March," said Sal, the owner. "You're back. Did you lose something?"

"No, Sal. I was wondering if I could use your phone. Mine broke." That was somewhat truthful.

"Not a problem."

Hal used the phone on the counter and dialed a number he knew by heart.

"Joey. Hal March."

"Hey."

"You remember that blue SUV you're taking care of for me? Can you get it ready? I'll be over within the hour."

"Not a problem. It'll be ready for you."

"Thanks." He hung up and spied Derek, the cook, getting ready to leave.

"Derek, want to earn a quick hundred?"

"Always."

"I just need you to drive me to Revere."

"Heading that way, myself. That'll be an easy hundred."

An hour later, Hal was driving Ray Burton's SUV down I95 toward New York. Ray had left the vehicle when he headed for the time portal in Arizona. Hal said he'd take care of it, and he had, making sure it was in good running condition and renewing Ray's Florida registration. Before he left, Hal stopped at a phone store and bought a cheap burner phone. The NSA would be watching all of the usual ways Hal could leave the country, so he would have to call up a few people. His years in journalism had produced numerous contacts in virtually every field.

Hal stopped at a few coin shops in Connecticut on his way to New York and bought some English currency pre-1960. He had a feeling he'd need it. Unfortunately, none of the stores had much, so he hoped he'd find another one in London that might have more.

Three days and a $5,000 pay-off later, Hal was nestled in a small cabin on a freighter bound for England.

Maybe now, he'd find out why he had lost all contact with Ray and Natalie.

Chapter 2

NEW YORK CITY

Alexander Frost just wanted to go home.

This was somewhat ironic, as he had never actually left home.

On June 3rd, 1973, Alex walked out of his one-bedroom apartment in the Bronx, on his way to the school five blocks away, where he taught 7th-grade history.

But that day would be like no other.

Halfway to the school, he saw Butch Farmer, one of his students, running down an alley. The boy was not going in the direction of the school, and Alex was worried. Butch had a tough home life, with a nonexistent father and an overworked mother. Alex had tried hard to keep Butch on the straight and narrow and had succeeded to some extent. But Butch was prone to getting into trouble, and this looked like one of those times.

Alex turned down the alley and saw Butch enter an abandoned warehouse. He was probably going inside to smoke pot. Alex sighed. He was going to have to go in after him.

Alex reached the door he had seen Butch go through. Or rather, it had once been a door. Now it was just fragments of the door hanging off some rusted hinges.

"Butch? Are you in here? It's Mr. Frost."

No answer.

"Come on, Butch, talk to me. I saw you come in. I promise you're not in trouble."

He heard scuffling on the other side of the dark room. Butch or a rat?

"Butch?"

Alex took three steps and fell into a void. He dropped about ten feet and landed hard on the concrete below. It took a minute for him to get his bearings. Then he realized that the floor must have rotted away, and he had fallen into the basement.

He sat up gingerly and felt himself for blood or bruises. No discernable blood, but plenty of bruises. He stood up and dusted himself off. There was a lot of dust. He had heard that the building had been abandoned decades earlier. He would have to talk to his assemblyman about getting it razed. Some young kid could fall into the hole and kill himself. Alex had a feeling Butch was familiar enough with the building to avoid the same spot he had just fallen through.

It was almost pitch black, with the only light being a hint coming through the hole in the floor above him. But it wasn't enough to see by, and Alex was without a flashlight. He called out to Butch. Nothing. Either the kid was ignoring him, or he was already gone.

Alex felt a rising fear. How was he going to get out? He could barely see a foot in front of his face, and that was only while he stood under the hole. Beyond that was only blackness.

He had to find a way out. There had to be stairs someplace. He slowly made his way over to where he assumed the outer wall to be. Then he tripped over something and landed hard, with his head bouncing off the concrete.

He groaned and pushed himself to his knees, then felt his forehead. It was sticky. Blood that had almost dried? Had he passed out?

There was light. It was a hazy light, but it wasn't there when

8

he tripped. He stood up slowly and looked behind him to see what he had tripped over. Nothing. In its place was a wall. Where did that come from? In fact, there were walls all around him. He was in a room. It couldn't have been larger than 8' by 8', and it was full of junk. There were boxes and crates stacked to the ceiling. He couldn't tell what was in the boxes, but it didn't matter. Next to him was a door.

This is so strange, he thought.

He opened the door and walked through. Then he stopped suddenly and looked around. He was in the abandoned factory. Except it wasn't abandoned. He was still in the basement, but it was relatively clean, and it was in use.

Most importantly, it was light. He could see where he was going. Someone had packed crates and boxes in neat piles all over the room.

Alex saw stairs and made his way over to them.

Where was he? What had happened? He couldn't think of a scenario that made sense.

He climbed the stairs and emerged onto a busy factory floor. There were scores of men and women at stations all over the immense floor.

Besides the fact that none of this should be here, something else was odd about the scene.

"Hey, you!"

A big guy with bulging muscles approached him. The man was almost comical, dressed in 1920s or 1930s attire. He wore heavy boots, denim overalls, and a flannel shirt with the sleeves rolled up. He also wore a shop cap on his head.

"What are you doing here? And what the fuck are you wearing?"

Wearing? And then Alex looked around. Everyone was dressed in work clothes he had only ever seen in pictures from the early 20th century. He had on his teaching garb—a polo shirt, tan slacks, and sneakers.

Being honest was his best bet.

"I—I don't know."

The big man frowned.

"Honest. I have no idea how I got here. I'm not lying to you. I don't even know where I am."

The man's expression softened ever so slightly.

"Well, you ain't supposed to be here, so get out." The man motioned to a door.

"I will, thank you."

Alex hurried over and opened the door, then stopped short.

Everything was different outside. It was still New York, but it wasn't. It was a New York he had only ever seen in books and movies. Cars rolled past on the street, but they were all old. Was that a Model T? There were other cars he'd seen in museums, but he didn't know their names.

Alex felt a presence behind him. It was the big man.

"What are you waiting for?"

Alex turned to the man.

"I know this is going to sound strange, but what year is it?"

The man gave him a look as if he was trying to decide just how crazy Alex was. Something must have told him Alex was serious, so he responded with a sigh.

"1926."

Chapter 3

NEW YORK CITY—1926

Alex had been in New York of 1926 for two months. He still didn't understand what had happened, but it was clear that he had gone back in time. Back in time? Seriously? As impossible as that seemed, there was no denying the fact that he was now living in 1926.

This certainly wasn't his imagination, and if it was, it meant that he was in a dream he couldn't escape from. At first, the cars drew his attention, but then it was the people. They were all dressed in the garb of the 1920s—professional people, secretaries, newsboys.

The first few days had been the hardest. He had no money from that time period, and his clothes were not exactly in style. He had asked the big man, whose name was Bill, where he could find a place to get some clothes. He explained that he had no money. Bill directed him to a nearby church that fed and clothed the homeless. Bill also told Alex that they were hiring at the factory if he wanted a job. Alex had thanked him and hurried to the church, hoping that not too many people would notice his attire.

The church provided him with the clothes he needed, and the pastor even advanced him two dollars. That would pay for a room for a few nights at a boarding house and allow him to buy some food.

Alex tried his best not to panic. He didn't know how he got there, but there had to be a way home. Maybe it was in the room he had found himself in at the factory. He had to get back in there. He decided to take Bill up on his offer of work. Bill explained that it was hard to find workers with the prosperity of the time. Alex almost mentioned that the Great Depression was only a few years away but stopped himself. Something told him that keeping quiet was his best option.

The factory workers assembled telephones, and Alex was put at a table splicing the wires that attached the receiver to the phone's body. It was tedious work, but it allowed Alex time to try to figure out how he got there.

Ironically, one of the books Alex taught in his history classes was *Time and Again*, by Jack Finney. It had just come out three years before to much acclaim. He found it the perfect book for his students. It combined the excitement of time travel with an accurate picture of New York in the late 1800s and was a fun way to teach his students the history of their city.

But this wasn't a book. This was real. He had traveled almost fifty years into the past. The only good thing was that he was a New Yorker by birth. Once a New Yorker, always a New Yorker. His parents had grown up in the city—granted, on the rich side— so he had heard all the stories about the city in the 20s and 30s. It also meant that his parents were now alive as young people. As he settled in, he considered visiting his parents. Somehow though, he knew it wouldn't go well to announce to them who he was. Hell, they didn't even like him. Could he just observe them from afar? Did he even want to? He'd have to think about it.

There were some perks to living in 1926. Alex had already been to Yankee Stadium a couple of times and had seen Babe Ruth and Lou Gehrig play in person! As a lifelong Yankees fan, that was like dying and going to heaven. His 1973 Yankees sucked and had sucked for several years. The biggest news was the announcement in March that two of the Yankees starting pitchers had swapped wives. Not only wives but entire families, including the dogs. That said everything about where the Yankees were going that year.

Alex was tempted to place a bet and make a lot of money. After all, he knew that the Yankees made it to the World Series in 1926 but lost the series to the Cardinals in seven games. He could make a fortune. But, of course, he could also be dead if he did that. This was a tough crowd. Questions would be asked that he couldn't answer.

It was strange. Alex knew everything that would happen for the next fifty years—the Great Depression, the wars, the assassinations—but he couldn't tell anyone. He knew enough about the theory of time travel to know that you couldn't interfere with history. It wouldn't really be interfering, though, because if he told anyone what would happen in the future, he'd probably be committed to an insane asylum.

It had been a long two months. It was scary at first, then fascinating, but homesickness had set in. Now he just wanted to go home. He had gone back several times to the spot that had transported him, hoping that it would take him back. But it hadn't. On his breaks at work, he went down to the storage room so he could be close to his door to the future, hoping beyond hope that it would take him back, but it never did.

In 1973, it had been just beyond a pile of something that he had tripped over—probably bricks. In 1926, it was a storage room. That didn't make sense, though. If that room held a time portal, why weren't the people from 1926 getting caught in it? Was it possible that it could only go one-way? Because no matter how many times he entered the room, it wouldn't take him back to 1973. He didn't know how large or how precise the portal was, so he had inspected every inch of the room.

Alex was frustrated and depressed. Was he going to have to live in this time for the rest of his life? To make matters worse, he was beginning to think he was being followed. He had seen the same man several times over the past week. There was something about him that he couldn't put his finger on. It was his appearance. He was wearing the appropriate clothes for the mid-1920s, but, like Alex, the man seemed to be of another time. Was it someone who had gone through the same door from the future?

Alex was walking home from work one night after a tough day. No matter how hard he had tried, he couldn't fit in with the other workers. They all knew there was something "different" about Alex. As a result, he hadn't been able to make any friends. But, in some ways, it was just as well. What would he say to a friend? "Hi, I'm from the future. Do you want to hear about the things to come?"

No, he was better off remaining a loner. His "home" was one of the local flophouses. It was all he could afford in the beginning. Maybe in a few months, he could get an actual apartment.

A few months? That was depressing. He was going to spend the rest of his life in this place, and he knew it.

Alex was passing an alley when someone grabbed him, pulled into the darkness, and threw him to the ground. He hit his head on the pavement and yelped in pain. The alley smelled of urine and beer.

He looked up to find a man standing over him. It was the person he thought was stalking him. And he was pointing a gun at Alex. At least Alex thought it was a gun. It looked like nothing he had ever seen—even back in 1973. It had the vague shape of a pistol, but it was rounder. It reminded Alex of toy ray guns they sold when he was a kid. The man just looked at him without speaking.

"What do you want?" asked Alex.

"You're not supposed to be here," came the answer.

He was a small man who looked to be in his forties. There was nothing distinguishable about him except his ears, which were too large for his head. That, and the fact that he looked dangerous. It wasn't just the gun he was holding. It was his expression. The man was no stranger to violence.

"What?" asked Alex.

"You are not supposed to be here," the man repeated.

"No shit," answered Alex. He wasn't exactly sure what the man was getting at, but his answer covered most of the possible scenarios. Deep down, though, he knew. He wasn't supposed to be in this time period.

"You shouldn't have come here," said the man. "You shouldn't have used the portal."

"You think I did it on purpose? I discovered it by accident. I'd give anything to be back home now."

"It doesn't matter if it was on purpose or by accident," said the man. "It's too dangerous for you to be here."

"Dangerous? How is it dangerous for me?"

And then it hit him. The man didn't mean that it was dangerous for him. He meant that it was dangerous for the world that he was there.

"I haven't said anything or changed any history," said Alex. "I've been pretty invisible."

"It doesn't matter. Just the fact that you are here has changed history."

Alex felt a little pissed off now.

"What are you? The time police?"

"In a manner of speaking. I've been hired to hunt down everyone who has gone back or forward in time."

"Why?"

"Because you are not supposed to be here."

"You said that already—several times. So what are you supposed to do when you hunt them down?"

"Eliminate them."

Alex's eyes grew wide.

At that moment, a car honked on the street, someone yelled, and the stranger looked away for a second. Alex took that opportunity to kick the man hard in the leg. The man went down to his knees. Alex kicked him again, jumped up, and ran toward the street. As he reached the end of the alley and turned the corner, he was grabbed by a different set of hands.

It was a woman. She was young, probably in her thirties, with curly brown shoulder-length hair. Her expression was all business.

"Do you want to live?" she asked.

"What?"

"I said, do you want to live?"

"Yes."

"Follow me."

They ran down the street, turning several corners, before finally stopping behind an apartment building. The woman looked around carefully. Then, when she was satisfied that they were alone, she spoke again.

"Just answer my questions. I don't have time to give you explanations. Where are your things?"

"In my room."

"Is it close?"

"Yes."

"Is there anything there that you brought with you from your time?"

"My clothes and a small briefcase."

"Let's go. You need to get them. Make sure it's everything you brought with you. Everything."

They set off with Alex leading the way to his building. He noticed that the woman was wearing clothes appropriate for the 1920s, but generic. Nothing flashy.

They reached the flophouse, and Alex ran in while the woman waited on the sidewalk. He threw everything into a bag and was back out in barely a minute.

"Is that everything?"

"Yes."

"You're sure?"

"I said yes. What are we doing?" asked Alex, becoming annoyed.

"Just shut up and follow me."

The woman hailed a cab and instructed the driver to take them to Grand Central Station. She didn't say a word while they rode in the cab. When they reached Grand Central, she paid the driver, and they got out.

At a ticket window, the woman bought two tickets to Atlanta. The train wasn't leaving for an hour, so she directed Alex to some seats that gave them a full view of the station. They sat, and Alex caught his breath.

"Ask your questions," said the woman. "But make them brief."

"What's your name?"

"Hanna."

"Where are you from? Or rather, *when* are you from?"

"2105."

"Where are you taking me?"

"To England."

"By way of Atlanta?"

"Yes."

"Why?"

"You haven't figured it out?"

"Obviously not."

"I'm here to save your life."

Chapter 4

SOMEWHERE BETWEEN NEW YORK AND ATLANTA—1926

Hanna Landers couldn't believe it. After all she had given to the Project, now they were shutting her down. No, that was too nice of a way to say it. It was the Project they were shutting down. Hanna, they were eliminating—an antiseptic word for killing.

Alex was in the seat next to her on the train. His eyes were closed, and he was breathing steadily. While he seemed at peace, his body said otherwise. He was twitching in his sleep. Considering all that he had gone through, it wasn't surprising. Hanna knew that she had come off as a bitch to him. Is that what time travel had done to her? Or was it just her reaction to the news about the Project? Alex had tried to ask her questions, but she wasn't ready to respond. She had too much to think about. She told Alex to get some sleep and promised that she'd answer his questions when he woke up.

She looked at Alex again and felt a wave of sadness come over her. It wasn't his fault that he was stuck in 1926. How frightening it must have been for him to suddenly find himself in an alien world. At least he went backward in time and not forward. He could relate to the world in a historical context. To find yourself suddenly fifty or sixty years in the future with the technology of that time would be devastating to anyone.

However, she knew that it was of little comfort to Alex. He was still in a foreign place and not by his choosing.

She would have to try to be more understanding when he woke up full of questions. After all, she was once a nice person. However, twelve years of travel to strange and sometimes violent times had changed her.

Hanna tried to think back to the excitement she felt when she was picked as one of the six "travelers." She was only 23 at the time, the youngest of the group, and full of youthful optimism. Just imagine the subtle changes that could be made in the past—and not noticed—that could benefit humankind in the 22nd Century. She and her colleagues couldn't initiate any of those changes. Theirs were strictly scouting missions to observe and write reports. Later travelers could be the ones to "fix" the past.

But things didn't work out as planned. As far as Hanna knew, she was the only one of her fellow travelers still alive. She had seen the reports. Jim—nicknamed "Uncle" Jim—had died of cancer in 2021. Alan Garland also died in 2021, but he was killed by the NSA. Herb Wells was shot and killed in 1870. A lover's quarrel had been his demise. Hanna wasn't surprised. She had always questioned Herb's ability to stay detached. Max Hawkins was blown up in London in World War II. The word was that Simone, the other female traveler, might have committed suicide, but that wasn't confirmed. No one had heard from her in a long time. That made Hanna sad. She and Simone had become close during training.

Who could have known that when she sent back reports telling the Project team that the Time Travel Project was too dangerous to the world, they would take her so seriously that they'd want to kill her? But that's precisely what happened. Although the messages she got from Tony said that she wasn't the only one who thought that way. The Project had received similar evaluations from all of the other travelers.

Tony also said that the Project had been taken over by a more cautious branch of the NSA. They recognized the dangers inherent in time travel and had said that enough was enough—the Project had to quietly go away. The implication there was clear. Anytime the government wanted something to "quietly go away," anyone connected with it needed to disappear, as well.

Tony was Hanna's last link to the Project—and he had gone rogue. It was the only way he was able to stay alive. They had shut down the Project headquarters and taken the scientists somewhere. Tony was sure they'd been killed. But he was the lucky one. He'd woken up that morning with stomach issues that had kept him in the bathroom for over an hour. When he finally arrived at the Project's building, Tony knew something had happened, and he turned around and went to a covert place he knew. He put everything he had learned into a package and, when he felt he was safe to do so, visited the drop spot that had been set up with Hanna.

She had the package now, and it contained some scary information. Her life was in danger—but hers wasn't the only one.

New technology allowed the Project to track everyone who went through a portal, intentionally or accidentally. The portal left a residue on the travelers that allowed them to be tracked using this new technology. Tony had told her that luckily, they could tell the difference between animal and human travelers. Otherwise, they would forever be searching for millions of animals that had wandered through the portals.

Tony also told her that there were more than a dozen accidental travelers still living in their various periods. Others had either been arrested and locked away in prison or taken to an insane asylum. They would die with no one believing a word they said.

The NSA of the 22nd Century had sent four assassins back in time to find the dozen or so travelers they felt needed to be eliminated. She had just experienced her first one. No one said she had to rescue travelers. After all, she was a target herself. She just felt it was the right thing to do.

Hanna was sorry she had ever gotten involved with the Project, but she couldn't think about that now. After finding Alex, she now had to go to Saxmundham, England in the late 1950s. But first, they had to find a portal in Atlanta. That portal would take them further back in time but would lead to another one that would bring them to 1959. From there, they could make their way to England.

If the portal still worked. If any of them still worked.

Portals were known to degrade to the point of just shutting down. In the Project's research, they had determined that if a portal's time range increased, it meant that the portal was in the process of degrading. For example, if a portal was supposed to lead to 1959, and suddenly the range increased from 1957 to 1961, it meant it was getting close to shutting down. The Portal Finder indicated that the two she was looking for were still active. But for how long? If either of these two portals shut down, she wouldn't be able to help the two unauthorized individuals in England, and they would be on their own. She had imprinted their names on her brain.

Ray Burton and Natalie O'Brien.

Chapter 5

LONDON, ENGLAND — 2023

The journey to England had been uncomfortable, but Hal had traveled in worse conditions. A week in his tiny cabin on the freighter was nothing. When he arrived in England, he walked from the docks to a bank and changed most of his U.S. money for English money. He then hailed a taxi that took him to a couple of coin stores to buy some pre-1960 currency, then to Liverpool Street Station, where he purchased train tickets to the town of Saxmundham. He would have liked to have stayed a night in a nice hotel, but he couldn't afford to have his credit card out in cyberspace. Even if he paid in cash, he would have to put his credit card on file. Besides, the place in Saxmundham was comfortable.

Hal slept most of the journey from London to Saxmundham and arrived refreshed. Then, as he usually did, he walked from the train station to his house.

His house was a complicated situation and one that nobody would ever believe. It was purchased by Ray Burton (going by the name of Ray Bean) in 1958. Ray and Natalie had arrived in Saxmundham in 1958, by way of Hollow Rock, Arizona in 1870; San Francisco in 1969; and London in 1942. Working with a law office that he knew was still there in 2021, Ray bought the house and left instructions to turn the house over to Hal March in 2021. He also left a large sum of money for a manager to keep the property in good condition. The current lawyers in the firm were shocked that a Hal March really existed and were excited to finally pass on the documents sixty years later.

Hal normally journeyed to England to visit the house every two months to check his messages from Ray. There was usually a pile of papers awaiting him. But when he had received no communication from Ray six months earlier, he had stepped up his visits. Each visit revealed no new messages and resulted in more anxiety. What had happened?

Maybe Ray and Natalie had moved on. But wouldn't they have left a final message? If there was nothing from them today, he would have to do a little research on them and their time in Saxmundham—something he had held off doing so as not to draw undue attention to him or them.

Hal unlocked the front door, went in, and stopped. Something was wrong, but he couldn't put his finger on it. Someone had been there. That wasn't good. He didn't get the sense that there was anyone there now, but they had been. He pushed the door open wider. All was quiet. The house smelled musty, but it always smelled musty. What was it? He took the 9mm out of his backpack just to be safe. One of the advantages of being smuggled into the country was not giving up his gun.

He entered the house slowly. Hearing nothing, he quietly checked the rooms. There was nobody in them—but someone had been there. His bed in the main bedroom had been slept in. There was an empty soup can in the sink and a dirty pot. Whoever it was had only stayed one night. Then he saw the back door. It had been jimmied. That's how they got in.

Hal cautiously made his way down the cellar stairs. His close call with the NSA in Boston was still with him, making him overly jumpy. He stopped at the bottom of the stairs. Whoever entered the house had searched it for something. Local thieves or someone else? Papers that Hal had sent through the portal untouched by Ray had now been rifled through. Someone had read them. He sat down and considered the situation.

The house wasn't a random purchase. Using the Portal Finder, Ray learned that the basement contained a time portal. All portals were one-way only, and this portal emptied out in 1958 or so. Hal would send items through the portal. Ray would find them and respond by leaving things for Hal in a designated spot in the basement. So there would always be something new waiting for him. Until recently.

He saw something shiny in the corner of the room, near the entrance to the portal. Hal walked over and picked it up. It was a $5.00 coin—octangular shaped with a date stamped on it that read: 2116.

It belonged to a time traveler!

Chapter 6

Who had been in his house, and why? The fact that the person was still carrying money from the 22nd Century told him that he wasn't a long-time traveler. Why would a traveler even have money from his time? One would think they would be required to leave everything behind before embarking on their adventure.

Unless it served a purpose. Maybe on rare occasions the travelers needed to prove to someone where they were from. It would go against the rules that Ray had explained to him, that the travelers couldn't bring attention to themselves. But maybe a unique situation existed that would require it? Or perhaps it was just a good-luck piece.

If the traveler was in his house, it was to go through the portal. Was that related to why Ray had stopped corresponding?

There was still no sign that Ray had left anything for Hal. Well, he'd start his investigation tomorrow. Today he had to clean the house. It smelled musty and damp. He also had to fix the back door.

He went to the local pub for dinner, then stopped by a small store to pick up some essentials for the length of his stay. But, how long *was* he going to stay? Eventually, the NSA goons were going to track him down. His original intent was to leave this century altogether and join Ray and Natalie. But since he still hadn't heard from them, he was unsure if he wanted to make the journey.

Joining Ray and Natalie wasn't a decision he had come to lightly. He knew that once he went through the portal, the chances of him ever seeing his home again were slim at best. But with the NSA after him, what did he have to look forward to at home? And what if he arrived and Ray and Natalie weren't there? What would he do then? He would never be able to find another portal. He'd be stuck in England in the late 1950s.

He thought back to the day Ray arrived at his office looking for information on Stan Hooper, an ex-employee of Hal's who had disappeared ten years earlier. Hal was skeptical but fascinated when the talk eventually turned to time travel. When theory turned to reality, and Ray went through the portal in Hollow Rock, Arizona, Hal agreed to be Ray's contact in the 21st Century. As for going through the portal himself, he never gave it any consideration. Until now.

When Hal learned that James Robards, the former editor of *Time Magazine*, had been murdered, he knew he was next. Robards had come across Ray Burton's story and had written about it. Hal had reached out to the retired editor to talk to him about time travel and warn him about the NSA. Now he was dead, and Ray and Natalie were missing.

He had to find out what had happened to them.

Hal slept that night with his gun at his side. He was no longer trusting of anyone or any situation. And he was pretty sure it wouldn't take the NSA too many days to track him down.

The next morning, Hal made himself some toast and tea. He didn't have much appetite these days. Besides, he was anxious to start his research on Ray and Natalie.

He began his search with copies of the village newspaper to see if there were any articles on the disappearance of Ray and Natalie Bean, the pseudonyms they had used. Of course, no one they had befriended in the late 1950s would be alive today. Or if they were, they would be very old.

Hal spent the morning at the library looking through old issues of the local paper. Nothing before 1965 was online yet, and Hal was pretty sure they wouldn't have stayed that long. So, he began with the date in 1958 when they had arrived and worked his way forward. Luckily, the newspaper was only published weekly at that time, so he could go through them quickly.

Hours later, he gave it up. He was into 1962, and their names hadn't appeared once. They had done an excellent job of staying out of the spotlight. But, that just made it harder for Hal. He had learned a lot about Saxmundham of the late fifties and early sixties, but nothing that would help him.

It was late afternoon, and Hal could use a beer. He thanked the librarian for letting him do his research, then he left. It was a dreary day outside. Rain was in the forecast, but it hadn't begun yet. It was a short stroll to his favorite pub. He walked in and greeted the old-timers who made up most of the late afternoon crowd. They had come to know Hal over the past couple of years during his visits, so he no longer felt like an outsider.

He greeted his waitress, a husky middle-aged woman with a deep voice and an accent he couldn't understand.

"Like a pint?" she asked. Hal understood that. It was anything beyond that simple question that would throw him.

"Yes, please."

He looked around. A couple of the men sitting at the bar looked to be in their eighties, at least. Hmmm. He'd met them before but couldn't remember their names. The waitress brought his pint, and he picked it up and moved to the bar.

"Hey, chaps," he said, greeting them.

"Ah, it's the American. Back again, are you?"

Wilfred. That was his name. He was glad he remembered.

"I am, Wilfred. Hey, I have a question for you. How good is your memory?"

"If you want to know what I had for breakfast, I couldn't tell you. But, if you want to go back a few years, there's nothin' wrong with it at all."

"Well, good. Because I need you to go way back."

"Okay, try me."

"The late fifties."

"That's way back, but what do you want to know?"

"Were you living here?"

"Been here my whole life."

"Good. You know the house I own, right?"

"I do," said Wilfred. "I knew the previous owners," said Wilfred.

Hal's heart raced.

"That's exactly the information I'm looking for. It was Ray and Natalie Bean, right?"

"Twas. A nice couple. She was quite the looker. Very friendly. She worked here, you know. Served drinks. Had all of us guys dreaming about her. She was younger than him. But he was a nice enough bloke, too. But I know that she fancied me."

"Do you..." began Hal.

"Funny thing about her," continued Wilfred. "About ten years back, I saw a movie with an actress who was also named Natalie. I can't remember her last name. But, it looked just like her."

"O'Brien," said a man who had just sat down. He was completely bald and was about thirty years younger than Wilfred. "Natalie O'Brien. We all got sick of you talking about how she looked like this other Natalie you knew. That actress, she disappeared. Was never seen again."

"She did look like her," said Wilfred, insulted that the other man laughed at him. "What would you know anyway? You weren't even born when I knew the Beans."

He turned back to Hal.

"So, what do you need to know?"

"From what I understand," said Hal, "they disappeared and never came back. Do you know anything about that?"

"I do. They didn't disappear. I reckon they moved to Australia."

"You're sure?" asked Hal.

"Nothin' wrong with my hearing. I heard them myself. They were talking about it right here in the pub. I don't think they wanted anyone to hear, but I heard it. It was right after the other couple showed up."

"Other couple?"

"Yeah. Kinda strange. They seemed nervous. Always looking around."

"Do you remember their names?" Hal knew that was too much to ask.

"Nah, but the gentleman's name started with an A. I think his name was Aleck or Alex. They showed up, and a few days later, they were all gone. The four of 'em."

Who were the others? This added a whole new aspect to the situation.

"Mighta been another one with them, too. Can't remember that. I'll tell you one thing," he continued. "They left fast."

He took a swig of beer.

"It was like someone was after 'em."

Chapter 7

SOMEWHERE BETWEEN NEW YORK AND ATLANTA—1926

"Can you answer some questions now?"

Hanna looked over at Alex and smiled.

"You're awake."

He returned the smile.

"No, I'm just talking in my sleep."

"I want to apologize," said Hanna. "I probably came across as a bitch earlier."

"Kind of. But you also saved my life, so you're forgiven."

"You were twitching in your sleep," said Hanna.

"That's all? With all that's happened to me over the last couple of months, I'm surprised I wasn't in a fetal position with my thumb in my mouth. However, this was the best sleep I've had in a long time. I felt safe."

"I'm not a bodyguard by nature," Hanna said, chuckling softly. "But I've been traveling for twelve years. I've seen it all. I've learned self-protection the hard way."

"When you say 'traveling,' do you mean time travel?"

"I do. And I know your next question, so let me answer it now. I'm from Boston. I left there in the year 2105. That was twelve years ago in real-time."

"In aging time?"

"That's another way of putting it. I've gone all over the place in dozens of time periods, but my body continues aging the old-fashioned way. When I began, I was twenty-three. I'm thirty-five now."

"I'm thirty-eight," said Alex, "although I feel as if I've aged a hundred years in the last two months."

"I know the feeling. I've had enough of this," said Hanna frowning.

Alex caught a glimpse of moisture in the corner of her eye.

"Can you go home?"

"I'd have to find my way home, and that's complicated. But it doesn't matter. I can't go home. That person who tried to kill you also wants to kill me."

"I don't understand."

"The people who are in charge of what's known as the Time Travel Project need to shut it down, and they can't have people wandering all over time. So, they sent back a team of assassins to do away with people like you who came through accidentally and people like me who are a part of the Project. Although, I know that most of the others are dead. I couldn't go home even if I wanted to."

"Are there a lot of people like me?"

"Surprisingly few."

"Where are we going?" asked Alex.

"There are two people I have to warn. One of them entered a portal accidentally, just as you did. The other knowingly went through the portal to save her. It was a romantic gesture, but stupid. They are together in England in the year 1958, give or take a couple of years."

"Give or take?"

"I'll try to explain it. First: portals, such as the one you went through, are all one-way. That's why you couldn't take the same portal back to the time you entered it—as I'm sure you tried."

Alex nodded.

"Second: They are always in out-of-the-way places or hidden places. The scientists I worked with hadn't figured out why that is. They assumed it had something to do with energy levels—the more active the area, the less likely a portal would be there. Third: As for the 'give or take' comment, we've found that portals land travelers in a date range—usually about a year. So you could have landed here within a year either way of when you did. We've also come to realize that as a portal degrades—and they do eventually close down—the window widens. So if the portal you came through was degrading, your arrival window might have been something like 1925 to 1928. We still don't know how wide it gets before it vanishes altogether."

"How do you find the portals?"

"With a Portal Finder."

"Of course."

Hanna laughed. "Seriously. That's what it's called. I have one with me. I'll show it to you when we get somewhere a little more private."

Alex thought for a minute, then asked, "How many portals are there?"

"Hundreds ... thousands. I don't know. They are all over the world but in different time periods. For example, when I last checked, there were just eight portals in the U.S. But that's eight portals that we can access in this time period. At a different time, there might be more or fewer than that. Let's say you go to the year 1832. There might be a whole different batch of portals, taking you to completely different periods. And those portals would be in different locations than the eight available to us now. Factor in all the regions of the world and all the centuries and...."

"You need a roadmap," said Alex.

"Yes. Oddly enough, I have one," replied Hanna. "It's far from complete, and really only a sketch. But from the time I left until now, the scientists back home were able to devise one based on new technology they were using and by the reports the travelers filed. My friend, Tony, sent me one."

"Sent you one? How? UPS?"

Hanna laughed again. Alex found himself attracted to the laugh. It was soft and kind. He was seeing a completely different Hanna than the one he first met.

"No," she said. "We have contact points at certain portals where he sends me information through the portal. I can respond by leaving something for him. He will find it the next time he visits the portal."

"But how…" started Alex.

"How are they in order? Why couldn't he send something one day and it arrives on March 1st, then he sends something the next day, and it arrives six months earlier?"

Alex nodded.

"We don't know. It just happens sequentially. People going through don't necessarily do it sequentially, but inanimate objects seem to. There's a lot we don't know. And I'm afraid we never will."

"Why?"

"Because they are not just sending assassins to eliminate the travelers, they are shutting down the whole Project and wiping out everything we created. I don't mind being shut down. Time travel is too dangerous, and it's good that someone realized that. But I do mind the assassins they sent to eliminate anyone who might be a threat. Like you and like me, and like the people I have to find … Ray and Natalie."

"And we have to warn them?"

"Not just warn them," replied Hanna. "We have to team up with them."

"Team up?"

"Individually, any one of us can be killed by the assassins. As a group, it'll be a lot more difficult. We can plan and watch each other's backs. From the information Tony sent me, Ray and Natalie are self-reliant. And you have to be tough to survive time travel. So far, they've survived."

"One last question … for now," said Alex. "Will I ever get home?"

Hanna looked down at her hands.

"Honest answer?"

"Yes."

"Probably not."

Chapter 8

They rode in silence for a while, lost in their thoughts.

It was a mixture of sadness, fear, and curiosity for Alex. He knew what "probably not" meant. It meant "not." So, he was never going home. For the first time in years, he was happy that he had no family. He'd never found the right woman to marry, and he had no siblings.

Technically, he did have family. Both parents were still alive, but he never talked to them. They lived in another world. They were wealthy beyond most people's dreams, landing on the "Top 50" richest people in America list every year for as long as Alex could remember.

He had grown up privileged but hated that life. When he refused to follow in his parents' footsteps and work in the family business, they all but disowned him. They refused to pay for college. So, he paid for it independently, with grants, scholarships, and working every hour he wasn't studying. After college, he got a job teaching in New York. Alex hadn't talked to his parents in ten years and had no desire to. His disappearance wouldn't be missed.

He was dating someone, but it wasn't serious. She might wonder why he stopped calling her, but eventually she would start dating someone else. He missed some of his students, but it was just a job.

So, what was he sad about? Leaving behind the familiar, maybe?

The fear part was easy. It was the fear of the unknown. Of course, that was what most people were afraid of. His unknown, however, was lightyears beyond most people's "unknown."

But curiosity was the overriding emotion. He was looking forward to the adventure he had just embarked on. Well, minus the assassin. Despite the odd way that he met Hanna, and his initial judgment of her, she was intelligent and kind. And she truly cared about others. She didn't have to save him, just as she didn't have to find this Ray and Natalie couple. But she was putting her life on the line for others.

Yes, he was more curious than sad or afraid. He suddenly realized that he was excited to see what came next.

He glanced over at Hanna. Her eyes were closed. Was she asleep or lost in her thoughts? She looked so tired. Hanna said she had been traveling for twelve years. She looked it. She might have been only thirty-five, but the lines of exhaustion in her face told a different story. He didn't know anything about time travel, except that he was in the middle of it, but if Hanna was an example of what that life did to people, it was no wonder that most of her traveling friends were dead. Shutting down the program was probably the right thing to do.

Eliminating the travelers was not.

*****

Hanna's thoughts were different. She felt no excitement or curiosity for the task that lay ahead of her. Maybe she was just too jaded and too tired. Twelve years of lying. Twelve years of secrecy. Twelve years of never being able to express her honest thoughts and feelings. Hell, twelve years of no sex.

Unlike the deceased Herb Wells, she took her job seriously.

Having sex could easily impact history and the future in so many ways. Emotional ties could lead to questions she wouldn't be able to answer or would feel obligated to answer. It could take her to some very dark places. What if she got pregnant? That could throw everything upside down. Like so many other things she had to give up, sex wasn't an option.

Not that she hadn't been tempted many times. Maybe that's where her bitchy personality derived—self-preservation. She couldn't allow herself to have feelings. But her feelings had just come out when she was talking to Alex. Why was that? It was because Alex was a fellow traveler. He was the first traveler she had met over the twelve years. Granted, it wasn't his decision to travel, but he was here, and there was no reason for her to hold anything back. It was refreshing.

Hanna suddenly wondered about her appearance. Did she look as tired as she felt? Why did she suddenly care how she looked? She glanced over at Alex. Was he the reason?

She needed sleep. It had been so long since she had managed a restful sleep. It worked for Alex, having Hanna at his side. Maybe it could work for her, too.

She closed her eyes and fell into a deep slumber.

*****

They arrived in Atlanta in the dead of night. They had both been awake for several hours and felt refreshed, or as refreshed as they could feel under the circumstances.

At Hanna's urging, Alex told her about his life, his interests, and the story of how he entered the portal. Then, she asked him how he had survived being in a different era. Although she asked it innocently, Alex couldn't help feeling that she was trying to determine how tough he was. Could he be counted on when things got sticky?

Before he had a chance to ask her questions about her travels, they were in Atlanta.

They left the station and walked along the dark street. There were other people from the train on the road, so they felt somewhat safe. But with the assassin out there, they constantly looked over their shoulders. They were sure that the man hadn't followed them to the train, but they also knew that he'd eventually be on their trail again.

"Do you know where we're going?" asked Alex.

"Not yet. We have to find someplace quiet where I can check the Portal Finder. If anyone sees me looking at something with blinking lights, it'll draw too much attention to ourselves."

"No, I mean where the portal is going to take us."

"Oh. It's going to take us to Atlanta, of course. The year will be 1863."

"You're kidding."

"No. And, yes, I realize that it's in the middle of the Civil War. Luckily, the entrance to the next portal is only twenty or so miles away. That one takes us to 1959. I planned it so that I could find a portal that took us to the right time. All we need to do is get to England."

"That's all?"

"What do you mean?"

"I'm a history teacher. Atlanta was a major city for the Confederate Army. There will be troops all over the place. Neither of us sounds Southern, so if we get stopped, they might shoot us as spies."

"Too bad I didn't find a Northern portal," said Hanna. Alex thought that she didn't sound overly concerned about their situation.

"It wouldn't matter. They would probably shoot us as spies too."

Alex suddenly doubted that they'd ever make it to England.

"I can put on a decent Southern accent," said Hanna.

"Yeah, well, I can't. I'd sound like the Beverley Hillbillies."

"The what?"

"Never mind. I'll let you do all the talking."

They found a secluded spot, and Hanna removed a device from her backpack. The shape reminded Alex of a vase. It had a small screen surrounded by lights and switches. She flipped one of the switches, and a series of lights began to blink.

"What happens if the batteries die?" asked Alex.

"It doesn't use batteries," said Hanna. "It has a crystal inside that never needs charging."

"Can it break?"

"I read in a report that one of them broke. But the traveler was dying and not going anywhere, so it didn't impact him. He tried to fix it but wasn't able to."

"So if yours breaks, we're screwed."

"You might say that. But luckily, the Finders are well made, so I don't think we have to worry."

Alex watched with fascination as Hanna pressed buttons and made adjustments. He remained quiet as she worked. On the screen was a map. With each adjustment, the map changed.

"How far away can you pinpoint a portal?" he asked as she finished her adjustments.

"I can find them worldwide," she answered. "The farther away it is, the more general the location. As you get closer to a portal, you can fine-tune its location. Yesterday from New York, I knew it was in Atlanta. Now I know where in Atlanta. As we get closer to it, we can find its precise location."

"I'm impressed," said Alex.

"You should be," said Hanna. "You didn't have anything like this in 1973."

"No kidding."

"The portal is on the other side of the city," said Hanna.

"Maybe we can find a hotel until morning."

"I still have money from this time," said Alex. "We may as well use it up."

"Save some of it," said Hanna. "We might find a coin shop, and maybe we can buy some money from the Civil War era."

"Confederate money," added Alex. "Union money might not go over too well."

"Good point."

They found a hotel a few minutes later and checked in as Mr. and Mrs. Alexander Landers, using a combination of their names.

When they were in the room, Hanna said, "You're going to have to come up with a new last name. You can't go through history as Alex Frost because you were around in the 20th Century as that name.

"I assume Landers is not your name," said Alex.

"It's not. Technically, we are supposed to change our name whenever we visit a new time, but we never do. So I just use this name wherever I go. It's not my real name, so it works. In some ways, because I've used it so long, it's become my real name."

"Why don't I change mine to Landers, as well? That way, we can travel as a married couple, which will make it easier if we go to some uptight areas."

"That's a good suggestion." Hanna looked around the room. It had two single beds, a desk, a chair, and a washbasin. The bathroom was in the hall. She pointed to the beds. "At least we don't have to deal with any awkwardness."

Alex smiled. He thought that the longer he was around her, he wouldn't mind some of that kind of awkwardness.

"Let's see if we can get a little more sleep," said Hanna. "Tomorrow might be a stressful day."

If we live through it, thought Alex.

Chapter 9

SAXMUNDHAM, ENGLAND—2023

Hal walked home from the pub wishing he'd brought an umbrella. The rain had begun while he was talking to Wilfred. It was drizzling when he left the pub, but now it was coming down at a good clip. He'd be soaked by the time he arrived home.

If Ray was going to leave, why wouldn't he have told him? And who were the two "friends" who showed up? Were they allies or enemies? Hal had to assume they were allies. Ray was no pushover. He had led a rough life as a correspondent, writing from all the major hotspots of the 1990s and early 2000s. And from what he read in Ray's writings to him, Hal guessed that Natalie was tough in her own right. So, no, if these two were not friends, Ray and Natalie would have taken care of them.

The two friends seemed nervous to Wilfred. That told Hal that someone might have been tailing them. But who? Either way, Ray wouldn't have left without telling Hal, so there must be a message somewhere in the house. Ray wouldn't have left it out in the open, so it was up to Hal to find it.

As he approached his house, he stopped. Something was wrong. He hadn't left any lights on, but he could see one on now. It was moving—a flashlight.

A crack of thunder. It was pouring now. The rain and black

clouds made the late afternoon seem like the middle of the night. Whoever was in his house needed a flashlight to see by. They couldn't risk turning on any lights. Well, they had shown their hand.

Hal ducked into a fish and chips shop across from his house. He had to think.

"Mr. March, what are you doing out without an umbrella?"

Mr. Patel was the owner of the shop. He was a friendly man originally from India but had lived in England for almost thirty years.

"I didn't think ahead, I guess."

"I can lend you one."

"It wouldn't help now, I'm afraid," said Hal, laughing.

Mr. Patel chuckled and asked if Hal wanted the usual.

"Yes, please." Waiting for Mr. Patel to make the takeout order would give him a little more time to think.

"Oh, your friends arrived."

"What?"

"Your two American friends. They stopped in and asked if that was your house. I told them it was. They said you gave them a key, and they would let themselves in."

"Ah, yes. I didn't expect them for another day."

"If I may say, they are not very friendly. Please don't take offense."

"I won't," said Hal. "You are right. They aren't very friendly. They are not really friends. More like business associates. In a weak moment, I told them they could stay with me for two nights, but I think I'm going to suggest that they stay in a hotel. I really don't want any visitors."

Whoever it was had broken in. It had to be the NSA, and they had come to kill him. He could leave now and not go back to the house, but what would that serve? And where would he go? No, he had to face them. He had his gun on him. These days, he didn't go anywhere without it. If Ray had left him a note, he didn't want them to find it.

Hal thanked Mr. Patel, picked up the food bag, and headed across the street to his house. The flashlight beam was still on in his living room. He'd go around to the back and enter through the kitchen door. What then?

There was only one choice.

As he passed the windows on his way to the back of the house, he could see the silhouettes of the two men. Hal set down his soggy bag of fish and chips and quietly opened the back door. He could hear them talking in the living room. He slipped into the kitchen and closed the door behind him.

Could he do what he was about to do?

He was a desperate man. He could do anything he needed to do.

Hal knelt on the floor and rested his gun hand on the table for support. Between being soaked from the cold rain and the nervousness, he was shaking. He put his left hand under the light switch next to the table and waited.

Hal heard the two men in the living room talking quietly.

"Where the hell do you think he is?"

"Shit, I don't know. Do you think the Indian guy in the fish and chips shop warned him?"

"Nah."

"We've got to get rid of him fast and get out of here. Do you know the way to the airfield?"

"Would you stop worrying?"

"I've gotta get a drink."

Hal heard the man walk toward the kitchen. As he entered, Hal flipped the switch. The room was suddenly ablaze with light. The man started to reach for his gun, then saw Hal aiming his pistol at him.

"I wouldn't," said Hal, speaking loudly. "Your friend can

hear us, and I suggest he comes into the kitchen now with his hands in the air."

"Or?"

"Or you are dead. Don't underestimate me. I'm on the run from you, and I know that you mean to kill me. If your friend comes in here, you both might live. If he doesn't come in by the count of five, you are dead. And then I will get him before he's out the front door. If I hear him at the front door before I'm finished counting, you are dead."

Hal put both hands on the pistol.

"One...."

"Mike, come in here."

"Two...."

"Mike!"

"Three...."

"Holy shit, get in here!"

"Four...."

The man in the kitchen ducked down and drew his gun. At the exact moment, Mike jumped through the entranceway, his gun blazing. Hal fired one shot at the man in the kitchen and heard a grunt. He ducked down below the tabletop and took two shots at Mike's legs. The man screamed and dropped to the floor. Hal took two more shots, and a growing bloodstain appeared on Mike's chest.

Hal stood up shakily and looked at the first man. He was dead. Hal's lucky shot caught the man in the temple. He felt for Mike's pulse. Nothing.

Hal dropped into a kitchen chair and set his gun on the table. He had just killed two men. Unexpectedly, he vomited. It landed on his shirt, pants, and shoes. He leaned over and threw up twice more onto the floor.

Ten minutes later, Hal pushed himself up from the chair and looked at the scene before him. Two dead bodies and lots of blood.

Had anyone heard the gunshots?

The rain was coming down in buckets, with the constant rumble of thunder. No one could have heard. There would be no passersby in this rain, there were no houses close by, and Mr. Patel kept his front door closed. He was pretty sure he was safe.

He went into the living room, turned on a lamp, then returned to the kitchen and turned off the light. He couldn't afford to have someone look in his window and see the mess. Then he changed his clothes. He'd wait another few minutes, just to make sure no cops came, then he'd clean up the mess. If the cops did come, he'd claim self-defense.

Hal ended up waiting almost an hour before he was satisfied that no one would come knocking at his door. During that time, he went through the men's pockets and pulled out anything that could identify them. As expected, they had NSA IDs. He cut the badges into tiny pieces, then threw them into the woods at the side of the house. He did the same to their driver's licenses and credit cards. When the men were eventually found, long after Hal was gone, there would be nothing to use for easy identification.

Then he began the cleanup. He dragged the men, one at a time, out the back door and put them in the shed behind the house. The rain was still coming down hard, which washed away the blood.

As he was returning to the house after taking the second man to the shed, he tripped. He shone his flashlight on the spot where he tripped. Something was protruding from the ground. It was a skeletal hand! He knelt and dug around the hand. It was attached to an arm. He wasn't going to dig the thing up, so he covered it with dirt. At some time in the past, a person had been buried there, and the recent heavy rain had exposed it.

And then he had a terrible thought. What if it was Ray? Or Ray and Natalie. That would explain why he hadn't heard from them. As much as he didn't want to do it, he grabbed a shovel and started digging. Finally, he was able to determine that there was only one body. It was impossible to know if it was Ray. He had seen skeletal remains before and knew it wasn't female.

So either it was Ray, and Natalie escaped, or it was someone else. He just had to assume it wasn't Ray. Hal quickly covered it up and went to the house. He still had a lot to clean up there.

Using towels, Hal soaked up as much of the blood in the kitchen as he could, then carried the towels out to the shed. He then scrubbed the blood off the linoleum floor with soap and water and followed with bleach. It took several hours, but when he finished, the kitchen looked like it had before the men showed up. The wall had two bullet holes, but they were low enough that he was able to hide them by pushing a chair against them. Next, he opened the windows to dissipate the bleach smell. By then, the rain was back to a drizzle.

Hal took a long hot shower and put on some dry clothes. He closed the kitchen windows and made sure everything was locked. It was time to go to the basement.

If Ray left him a note, he would find it tonight.

Chapter 10

Hal surveyed the basement to get an overview before beginning his search. But his mind kept going back to the two men he had killed. *He had killed two people!* The reality of that was almost more than he could fathom. He had not just killed two men, but two U.S. government agents.

He sat on the steps and took a breath. *Calm down. These men were going to kill you.* Hal breathed deeply. It didn't matter who they worked for. They were sent to kill him. It was him or them.

He was beginning to relax. The men didn't deserve to live. If they were willing to snuff out the life of another human being, then they had to be ready for someone to end their lives. The big question was whether there would be someone else coming after him. Probably. Once these two failed to check-in, others would be sent to find them and then finish the job. But it wouldn't be right away. Hal probably had at least a day or two, maybe longer. That might be enough time to … to do what? That would depend on what he found.

Ray *had* to have left something for him. When they had met a couple of years earlier, there was an immediate connection between them. That connection continued once Ray went through the portal. Their "portal" correspondence had brought them even closer. There was no way Ray wouldn't have left him a note. The only question in Hal's mind was whether the basement intruder had already found it. There was nothing he could do about that, so he just had to search for it with the assumption that the person didn't find it.

He stood up. It was time to go to work.

Soon after he had moved in, Hal hired a contractor to finish the basement. He wasn't worried about the man finding the portal. He had stacked furniture near the portal entrance and told the contractor to finish the basement only up to that point.

The room was filled with tables and file cabinets to keep everything in order. He was trying to keep accurate records of everything Ray left for him. Hal had already searched drawers, but it was cursory. He needed to go through them more carefully now. Had the person who was here found anything? Hal assumed that the person in the basement was a traveler who came to access the portal. But from where? The person must have had a Portal Finder. So, where did they come from? Was it one of the two travelers Ray said could still be alive, or was it someone else? A new traveler from the future? And if they specifically used this portal, were they following Ray and Natalie?

It was too much to think about. Whoever it was had rifled through the file cabinets.

If Ray had left Hal a message, it must've been in plain sight, right? If so, then maybe the traveler found it. But what if the message was in the batch of papers left by Ray before they disappeared? *Papers Hal had already filed.*

What had he filed? After all, it was many months ago. *Think!* What did Ray leave him?

There were his notes about life in England in 1958; a story of their first English Christmas; newspapers from the time; and a few items that would be considered antiques in the 20th century. Ray often left Hal items that he thought might become valuable. Hal didn't sell them. Instead, he featured them in his magazine. After he wrote the articles, he would donate the item to a museum if he felt it was museum-worthy or give it to Joyce. She was a valuable employee and deserved the little bonuses. She had been able to sell some of the items for an excellent price. Hal knew that Joyce had questions about the source of the objects but never asked. He was pretty sure she even suspected a time travel angle, based on Hal's correspondence with James Robards and having met Ray Burton, the man Robards wrote about in his time travel articles. However, she was smart enough not to ask.

Hal was content to write about the pieces in his magazine.

His magazine! He always left Ray copies of *Antiques, Etc.* When Ray finished with them, he always destroyed them—the fewer clues to time travel left lying around, the better. But the last issue Hal had sent through the portal was in the pile Ray had left for him. Why? What was the significance of that?

Hal hurried over to the file cabinet that had the items Ray had left. Hal's filing system was rather complicated. He filed Ray's notes in one cabinet and other significant things that he wanted to keep in order in another. The other items were filed all together by date. That's the file he went to. He opened the file and found the magazine. The edge of a piece of paper stuck out from the middle of the magazine. Why hadn't he noticed it before?

He pulled the paper from the magazine.

A note from Ray!

Chapter 11

ATLANTA, GEORGIA—1926

Despite having slept on the train, Alex and Hanna managed to get a few more hours in the hotel. They were up early and took turns in the tiny bathroom. There was no hot water, so they took cold showers and dressed quickly to warm up. The hotel had a restaurant, so they took the time to eat. The food was bland, but at least they had something in their stomachs.

They walked the streets of Atlanta in search of two stores: a coin store and a store that sold costumes. If they were going back to 1863, they would have to look the part. They would dress simply for freedom of movement, especially for Hanna. No bustles or girdles or hoop dresses. She would dress in a simple cotton dress like a farmer's wife. Alex, in turn, would try to look like a farmer, with baggy pants, a long-sleeve shirt, work boots, and suspenders. He already had some of the clothing from his work in the factory. It was similar to what they would wear in the 1860s.

Atlanta was a bustling city, modern for its time, with cars and streetcars filling the streets and pedestrians crowding the sidewalks. Despite having lived in 1926 for a couple of months and getting used to life in the 20s, Alex felt out of place in Atlanta. At least New York had a familiarity about it, despite the year.

Atlanta was foreign to him. The sooner they could leave, the better. But if he felt out of place in 1926 Atlanta, how would he feel about 1863 Atlanta?

They found the two stores they were searching for, and Alex spent most of his remaining money on 1860s Confederate currency.

"I don't know how much we're going to need," said Alex. "By 1863, the Confederate money was becoming almost worthless."

"We'll probably get there sometime around the middle of 1863," said Hanna. "This portal hasn't degraded, so it's a little easier to pinpoint a time. Does that help?"

"The earlier, the better where the money is concerned. We'll just have to take our chances."

"Hopefully, we won't be there long enough to worry about it," said Hanna.

"If arriving early in the year is a possibility, we can't forget to buy coats," said Alex.

Hanna made a face and said, "I've been doing this a long time. I know how to prepare."

She instantly regretted her response.

"I'm sorry, Alex. I didn't mean it like that. I guess I've been alone for so long and have only had myself to rely on. All these things are second nature. But unfortunately, what seems to have also become second nature is a prickly attitude. You didn't deserve that. I'm sorry."

Alex took her hand. "It's okay. I'll never understand all that you've probably had to go through these past twelve years, but I know it couldn't have been easy. So just know that while I don't have the experience you have, I'll help in any way. I don't want you to have to carry the load."

She looked him in the eyes and smiled.

"Thank you for understanding. I'm trying. It's strange for me even to be talking to someone about this. You may not be able to understand the complexities of it all yet, but just being able to talk to you is a great relief to me."

She left her hand in his. It felt good, and she was in no hurry for it to end. They walked into the coin shop, still holding hands.

They had their money and clothes two hours later and headed to the portal across town.

"What's the routine?" asked Alex. "Do we change clothes before going through?"

"When possible," answered Hanna. "It all depends on where the portal is. Normally, they are in secluded spots. But if the entrance isn't secluded enough, we have to go through and hope for the best. I never like doing it that way."

It took them another hour to find the portal.

"What is the worst portal you've ever gone through?" asked Alex.

"There was one in Canada near a lake. It was the early 1800s, and I was going forward in time about fifty years. I went through the portal and found myself underwater. In fifty years, the lake had grown significantly in size. Needless to say, it was a shock."

Alex laughed. "Well, let's just hope we don't come out in the middle of a firing squad."

Hanna had been surreptitiously checking the concealed portal finder as they walked.

"Around this corner," she said.

They turned the corner and stopped.

A lake.

"You've gotta be kidding," said Hanna. She looked at the Portal Finder again. "Luckily, it's not in the lake." She looked around. "It's in those rocks off to the side."

They climbed the rocks, following the directions given by the Portal Finder. Hanna was openly watching it now, as they were alone.

"Stop. It's in that hole."

There was a ten-by-ten hole between two boulders, about eight feet deep.

"Do we just jump in?" asked Alex.

"We do, but let's change first."

After they changed and had put their 1926 clothes in their backpacks, Hanna asked, "Are you ready?"

Alex wasn't sure. *Was* he ready?

"Are we allowed to hold hands as we go through?" asked Alex. "Not that I'm nervous or anything. I just want to make sure we get there at the same time."

Hanna said, "You bring up a good point. I've been doing this alone and have had no need to think about things like that. But you're right. Even if we go through within seconds of each other, we might land months apart. So keep bringing up questions like that. Please don't assume I know the answer."

"So, if we hold hands, are we guaranteed to arrive together?"

"Yes. That much I *do* know. As long as we are connected somehow when we go through, it sees us as one object. Are you ready?"

"I think so. Remember, the only other time I went through a portal, I didn't know I was doing it."

Alex took Hanna's outstretched hand.

"Let's do this," he said.

They moved to the edge of the hole.

"Here we g...." The edge of the hole was slippery, and Hanna lost her balance. Trying to catch herself from falling, she let go of Alex's hand and fell into the hole.

She was gone.

Chapter 12

"Nooo!" cried Alex.

Without thinking, he jumped into the hole after her.

He was standing at the bottom of the hole. Had anything happened? Did he go through the portal? It didn't feel any different. Alex knew that Hanna had made it through the portal. After all, he saw her disappear. But it all seemed the same to him.

Except that it was raining. A drizzle was coming down. He looked down at his feet. It must have poured because the water was halfway up his boots.

He heard men yelling. He slowly peeked out over the top of the hole. The lake was on his right, and the city of Atlanta was spread out in front of him. But it was a very different Atlanta than the one he had just been in. Some square brick buildings were within view, but many of the other buildings were made of wood. The roads were dirt and had become mud puddles in the rain. What had just been a bustling city was now tiny in comparison.

It was still busy but in a different way. Townspeople— primarily men—sat in store doorways smoking cigars, and groups of soldiers gathered on street corners. They seemed to be waiting for something. Other soldiers, some dressed in the gray Confederate uniforms and others with parts of uniforms, wandered the streets.

Alex knew that poverty plagued the Confederate Army

throughout the war, and it was on full display here. But there was something else. There was a look of despair in the faces of the men. Had something just happened?

It didn't matter. Alex's only priority was to find Hanna. He couldn't believe that they had become separated. What now? Did he arrive before her? Had she already been there for days, weeks, or months? If she had arrived before him, would she have gone ahead with the second part of her mission, to find the portal and try to find Ray and Natalie? No, she wouldn't do that. She would wait for Alex to arrive.

But what if he arrived before her? It meant that he would have to survive on his own until she got there. Could he do it? One word out of his mouth, and they would know that he was from the north. Could he put on a fake southern accent, an accent that would fool real southerners? Probably not.

Whatever he did, he was going to have to do soon. He was standing in three inches of water in a cold rain.

Alex suddenly had an idea, but he would have to get out of the rain to do anything about it. He climbed out of the hole, slipping once and covering himself with mud in the process. He reached back into the hole, grabbed his backpack, then went down the hill and wandered into the town. At least the large farmer hat he was wearing kept the rain out of his eyes.

He needed to find a store that sold paper and pencils. He passed one of the groups on the corner, listening for anything that would be useful. He heard the word, "Lee." They were talking about Robert E. Lee, but he couldn't get the gist of the conversation. Then he heard someone complaining about wanting to go back to their farm. They said they were tired of fighting a losing battle. Finally, as he was almost out of earshot, he heard the word, "Gettysburg."

That was it! That's why he saw so many signs of despair among the men. If this was 1863, it must be later in the year, after

Gettysburg and after the fall of Vicksburg—two significant defeats of the Confederate Army. The rain was cold, so it had to be autumn. He had to be extra careful. The soldiers would be tired and angry. That's why his idea was a good one. At least he hoped it was.

After wandering for close to an hour, he found what he was looking for—a store that sold writing supplies.

It was warm in the store, and a couple of men were sitting next to a woodstove.

"Hep ya?" asked one of the men.

Alex pointed to his throat and made a motion indicating that he couldn't talk. He mimed writing. One of the men pointed to a stack of notepads. Alex selected a couple of pads and pencils and brought them to the counter. He put a dollar on the counter, which the storekeeper scooped up without giving any change. Alex wasn't surprised. He knew that the Confederate money was becoming almost worthless at this point.

Alex wrote on one of the pads of paper:

Cain't speke. Looking for my wife. Her name is Hanna. 35 yeers old. curly brown hare. Have you seen her?

He was hoping that he wrote like an uneducated farmer.

"Run out on ya?" asked one of the men.

Alex shook his head.

"Can't hep ya. But check other stores. Maybe a saloon."

One of the other men said, "Wait a minute. There is a woman looking for her man. Cain't remember where she works, though."

That was encouraging. Hanna was here!

Alex gave them a wave in response and left the store.

His first test worked. They didn't seem suspicious.

Now he had to find Hanna.

Chapter 13

Hanna had been in Atlanta for over a month and now worked as a waitress in a restaurant. It was October 1863, and she hadn't seen Alex. It meant that she appeared before he did. How long was she going to have to wait for him? Luckily, the portal was strong, so it wouldn't be a case of waiting for a year, but several months was certainly a possibility.

She couldn't believe that she had slipped into the hole. She wasn't going to berate herself. It happened. Move on. She had dealt with mishaps before and had learned to think on her feet. Alex, on the other hand, was new at this. Would he be completely overwhelmed? She hoped not. He was intelligent, but was he ready to cope with something like this?

As soon as Hanna had come out of the portal, she put together a plan. She had been in the south before in her travels and could put on a somewhat decent southern accent. She knew that her first job was to see if Alex had made it there before her, so she used a story of getting separated from her husband on their way to Atlanta, and had anyone seen him? After two days, she determined that he wasn't there, so her next goal was to get a job since Alex had all the money in his backpack. The waitress job paid almost nothing, but the owners provided her with a small room. It wasn't much more than a closet with a bed, but it was a place to sleep while she was waiting for Alex to appear.

Word of the Confederate defeats at Gettysburg and Vicksburg had arrived around the same time Hanna had emerged from the portal. She had seen how it affected the soldiers and residents of Atlanta. Fights were breaking out almost every night on the streets. Sometimes they were fights stemming from differing political opinions, and sometimes they were simply out of anger and frustration.

The owners of the restaurant, James and Mattie Walker, warned Hanna not to walk the streets, even during the day. But she had to find Alex. The owners understood her need to find her husband, and James slipped her a derringer to hide in her coat for protection.

Hanna spent time every day when she wasn't working looking for Alex and spreading the word that he might show up. She avoided the soldiers as much as possible, but the other shopkeepers promised to keep an eye out for him. Finally, after a month of spreading the word, Hanna was optimistic that Alex would be noticed by someone and sent her way.

*****

She was on her way back to the restaurant after running an errand for James and Mattie when she turned a corner and bumped into a group of three soldiers. She fell to her knees. One of the soldiers helped her up.

"Well, hello, pretty gal," said one of the men. "You have to be more careful."

"My apologies," said Hanna. "Thank you for helping me up."

"I should get a kiss for that."

Hanna looked at the man and smiled.

"Thank you again, but I only kiss my husband."

"Well, now, I heard rumors that your husband isn't around. He's probably shacking up with some toothless wench on the outskirts of town."

The other two soldiers snickered.

"Please let me get back to my job."

"After I get my kiss." The man puckered his lips and stuck them out in an exaggerated manner.

Hanna tried to walk around him but was blocked by the other two.

"I think he deserves a kiss," said one of the others. "In fact, I think we all deserve kisses." He grabbed her arm and pulled her to him. She smacked him in the mouth and stepped back, pulling the derringer from her coat.

"Whoa," said the first man. "There's no need for that."

"I think there is," said Hanna.

"Honey, that derringer has one shot, and there are three of us," said the man she punched. He was still holding his bloody lip.

"So, who wants to be the person I shoot?" asked Hanna.

Suddenly, the third man lunged toward her, and Hanna pulled the trigger. The man cried out in pain as a red hole appeared in his chest. The other two men dropped their rifles and attacked her, throwing her to the ground.

"You shot him!" yelled the man with the bloody lip.

"Leave her alone," came a voice from behind the men.

It was Alex!

He was pointing one of the men's rifles at the two soldiers.

"You won't shoot us," said the man with the bloody lip.

"I certainly will. Now get away from her."

"Hey, I know you. You're the mute. How come you can suddenly talk? And how come you have a northern accent? You're a spy."

While they were focused on Alex, Hanna picked up one of the

rifles and, holding it by the barrel, slammed the gun's stock against the head of the man with the bloody lip. Alex quickly turned his rifle around and hit the third man, who crumpled to the ground.

"Good timing," said Hanna, with a look of relief and happiness. "Glad you finally made it, but we have to go."

"Yeah, the whole Confederate Army is going to be looking for two spies," said Alex.

"I have to stop by the restaurant where I've been working and pick up my things," said Hanna. "I'm all packed. I also want to thank the owners for their kindness. What did he mean about you being mute?"

"I've been here for two days searching for you. Since I knew I couldn't pull off a believable Southern accent, I pretended that I was mute."

"That was good thinking. Now we have to go."

The two men they hit with the rifles were moaning. They would be up and sounding the alarm soon.

Alex and Hanna ran down the street. When they reached the restaurant, Hanna told Alex to wait outside. She ran inside and handed James his derringer.

"Thank you for the protection," she said. "Unfortunately, I had to use it. I also found my husband, but the men who accosted me are saying that we are northern spies. We're not, of course, but we have to run. They won't let us prove our innocence. I want to thank you both for your hospitality and your willingness to give me a job."

"Here," said James, handing back the gun. "Take it. You might need it. And here are some more bullets." He hugged her, as did Mattie, who had quickly put together a bag of food. "Take care of yourself."

Twenty minutes later, Hanna and Alex reached the edge of the town and began their twenty-mile trek to the next portal.

Chapter 14

They stayed on the road when possible, but they also knew they could encounter more soldiers. If they did, they would probably still be safe until runners from Atlanta spread the word about the two suspected spies.

"For someone new at this, you did well on your own," said Hanna.

"I won't say it wasn't scary," replied Alex. "But you helped prepare me. I jumped through the portal only seconds after you. It wasn't a case of thinking that we might show up here at the same time. It was more a case of knowing that if I hesitated, fear might take over."

They were walking along a road that was little more than a wagon trail. They had been traveling for a few hours when they saw a group of soldiers coming from the opposite direction. They left the road and hid in the woods until the soldiers passed. They took that time to eat some of the food that Mattie had given them.

Alex felt compassion for the soldiers. It was a group of fifteen bedraggled men that passed by. Three were still in full uniform, and the rest were clothed in tattered fragments of uniforms. Some had apparent wounds, and most had blood stains on their clothes. There was no need to wonder where they were coming from. They had the look of defeat about them. They had made the long trip south from Gettysburg.

"It's all so strange," said Alex when the men had passed. "I looked at those men, and so many different thoughts went through my head. In a matter of years, they will all be dead. Where we come from, their deaths will be ancient history and not even a footnote in history at that. They will have been totally forgotten. Will we be forgotten? Am I already forgotten? After all, I disappeared. One minute I was there, and the next, I wasn't. Will my life mean anything to anyone in the future?"

They were sitting under a tree.

"Probably not," said Hanna. Then, at Alex's look, she added, "I don't mean that facetiously. You'll be remembered for a while. Of course, if you had a family, you would be remembered even longer. But that's how it is. There's nothing we can do about that."

"But doesn't it make you wonder about…"

"Life and death? My purpose in life?" finished Hanna.

"Yeah."

"No, not really. Maybe that sounds shallow, but I don't think it is. Everyone wonders about their purpose at some point in their life. And then what happens after we die? Is there a heaven? Do we get reincarnated? Do we just die, and that's it? Nothing more? Honestly, I can't answer that. And if I can't answer it, why should I bother asking? One of the reasons I applied for this job was to experience something different. Because of what I would be doing, every day would be different from every other day. That excited me. As for what happens when I die? Let me be surprised."

"Have your experiences lived up to expectations?"

Hanna went quiet for a moment. Then, finally, she said, "No. Not really. I mean, certainly, I've seen things beyond the realm of most people's imagination. But when I reach a new time period, how long does that wonder last? How long until I tire of it? Look at where we are right now. We arrived, and I immediately had to find a job….."

"Because I had the money," interrupted Alex.

"Well, yes. That was the case this time. But do you have any idea how many times I've had to get a job and find a place to live? It's exciting to arrive someplace, but after a few days, reality sets in. Food and shelter trump all."

"What exactly is your mission?" asked Alex. "To find portals? To report from different decades or centuries? To learn from other times and cultures?"

"I wish it was something as lofty as learning from other times. Because there is a lot to learn. No, that was supposedly going to be someone else's job later. It was all coming in stages. My job is—or now, *was*—much less glamorous than that. Yes, part of it was to find and map portals. But more importantly than that, they sent my team to measure the effects of time travel on the body, mind, and emotions. We had the technology to go back in time, but did we have the physical, mental, or emotional stamina to do it."

"Based on what you've said so far, I'm guessing the answer is no?"

"Correct. It's an overload of the senses."

"Stressful?"

"That doesn't even begin to describe it. You have to stay one step ahead of things at all times. You have to anticipate. But how can you anticipate something foreign to you? That does a number on your mind and emotions. I can't tell you how many times I've closed down for days at a time, not knowing how to proceed. Stress makes its way to your body, as well. You don't eat well, and you're always tired. I heard that one of my colleagues—we called him Uncle Jim—died of cancer. Was that somehow a result of time travel? Maybe not the travel itself, but the strain on the body? Who knows?"

"Does it get lonely?" asked Alex.

"So lonely. You can't talk freely to people. You can't make friends with people. You can't...." Hanna felt herself blush.

Alex reached over and took her hand. Tears welled up in her

eyes. He gently pulled her close, and she rested her head on his shoulder. Alex put his arm around her, and she relaxed against him. After fifteen minutes, Alex felt her steady breathing. She was asleep.

Alex leaned back against the tree and closed his eyes. It was a warmer day than the last few and was almost summer-like. They needed the rest. They needed a chance to recharge—Hanna especially needed it.

They slept for hours.

When Alex awoke, it was dusk. Hanna was sitting across from him.

"Hey," she said softly.

"Hey. Sleep well?"

"You can't imagine. Thank you for holding me. It's been a long time...."

She finished her sentence by leaning forward and kissing Alex lightly on the lips. He put his arms around her and pulled her closer. Her kiss became more intense as she hungrily sought out his tongue with hers. He moved his hand up her side and slid it over until he could feel her breast through the thin cotton dress. After a few minutes, they took a breath, and Hanna rested her head against Alex's chest.

"Wow," said Alex.

"Yeah," said Hanna.

They stayed that way for a little while, then Hanna pushed away.

"Not to ruin the mood," she said, "but I have to find a bush."

"I'll be right here."

Hanna escaped into the trees, and Alex stood up. Maybe he should find a tree, as well.

He heard a rustling in the bushes near the road.

"Well, if it ain't the Yankee spy."

It was the leader of the three they had encountered earlier.

His friend with the bloody lip stood next to him, and six others were behind them.

"Where's your woman?"

"She left me."

"She left you? Not enough man for her?"

"She didn't like the idea of being on the run. And I'm not a Yankee spy."

"You talk like a Yankee, and you're not in uniform. So that makes you a spy."

"I moved south before the war. So I can't help it that I don't speak like a Southerner. But I'm not a Yankee. I haven't been one for a lot of years."

Alex knew that he wouldn't talk his way out of it. He'd hit the guy with a rifle stock. The man wouldn't forget that. Plus, they had come a long way. There was no way they were going back empty-handed.

"Too bad your woman ain't here to watch you hang."

Alex saw Hanna emerge from the woods behind the men. What was she going to do? She only had one shot in the derringer. Hanna might get one of them, but the rest would overpower her quickly. And then he knew what she was planning. She was going to take out a few of them at once. It would be up to Alex to move quickly when she did.

Hanna suddenly charged the group and barreled into the six men in the back. They were on a slight hill, and four of the six went tumbling. The two they had met earlier turned to see what was happening, and Alex dove at them and knocked them over. He picked up one of the rifles that had fallen to the ground and slashed down on the leader's head with the barrel. Next, he turned toward the second man and rammed him in the face with the end of the barrel. It hit him in his already injured mouth. The man screamed.

Meanwhile, Hanna picked up one of the other rifles and

pointed it at the two still standing men.

"Don't move!" she said menacingly.

"And everyone else stay on the ground," said Alex.

Everyone stayed quiet. Alex could tell that Hanna was trying to figure out the best course of action. She gave him a questioning look.

Alex did some fast math. They had been walking for about four hours, give or take. If the average person walked four miles an hour, it meant they had probably gone close to sixteen miles. Therefore, they probably only had about an hour to go, and if they ran part of it, a lot less than an hour. So, the question was how to delay them from immediately following. Tying them up wouldn't work. Besides not having rope, getting that close to them would be too risky. They only needed a fifteen- to twenty-minute head start.

"Everyone strip down to your underwear," said Alex.

"I ain't wearing no underwear," said one of the men.

"Then strip down until you are bare-ass naked."

"I ain't gettin' nekked in front of a woman."

"She won't look. Throw your clothes in a pile. Shoes, too."

When no one moved, Alex pulled back the trigger with a click.

"I don't want to shoot anyone, but I will."

He pulled two more rifles away from the men.

The men slowly stripped. Two of them had ragged underpants, and the rest were completely "nekked" and covering their private parts with their hands.

"Now, Hanna is going to throw your clothes in the woods. We just need a little head start. For your information, we are NOT spies. We are just two people who want to go home."

While Alex covered the men with a rifle, Hanna picked up the clothes and ran into the woods. She threw the clothes behind rocks, under bushes, and onto tree branches. It took her three trips, and then she picked up one of the rifles when she was finished. Since the rifles only held one round apiece, they wouldn't get all the men if they chose to charge them, but the soldiers knew that at least two would be shot.

"We'll deposit your rifles up the road a ways. So, after you find your clothes, I suggest you get your weapons and head back to Atlanta," said Alex. "I promise you that you will never find us. We will disappear, and you'll wonder if we were just a figment of your imagination."

Hanna picked up the remaining rifles. They were heavy, so they wouldn't be able to take them very far, but it might give them the advantage they needed.

They left with half the men swearing at them and the other half running into the woods to find their clothes.

They dropped the rifles one by one along the path, then ran for about fifteen minutes. Finally, a little more than an hour later, they reached the vicinity of the next portal.

Chapter 15

Using the Finder, Hanna located the portal in a thick grove of trees.

"We're going to 1959?" asked Alex.

Hanna nodded.

"You nervous?" she asked.

"Kind of. I shouldn't be. I've done this twice before, although the first one wasn't intentional. The second one was frightening because we got separated. Neither one was run of the mill, so, yeah, I guess I'm a bit nervous."

"I have news for you," said Hanna. "There is no such thing as run of the mill. I may not show it, but I'm nervous every time I go through."

"Seriously?"

"Seriously. I shouldn't say this to you, but I think we're close enough now for you to get the full picture. Anything could go wrong. I'm most nervous about what's on the other side. What if I come out of the portal in someone's living room? These things are one-way. The exit could easily be in someone's house, and they would never know it. Suppose I'm caught by the local police and put in jail or sent to a psychiatric hospital? I could spend the rest of my life there. Our encounter with the soldiers is an example of the danger involved. It's tough when you go back into the 1800s. I've never been to the 1700s, but it's something that The Project wanted us to explore. I haven't been able to bring myself to do it, and I don't think any of my coworkers could, either. I've been afraid every day for the last twelve years. It's why I feel and look so ragged."

"I think you're beautiful." Alex knew he was taking a chance saying it.

"That's kind of you," she said in almost a whisper.

"I'm serious, Hanna." He took her hand. "I've never met anyone like you. It was worth falling in the portal to meet you." He kissed her lightly on the lips. She put her arms around him and hugged him tightly.

"And I'm glad you were honest with me," he added. "Yes, I'm nervous, but I'm happy going through with you."

"Thank you," Hanna said quietly.

"On another subject, my 1926 clothes will be out of place in 1959," said Alex, "and I certainly can't wear these clothes. So I'm probably better off with my original 1973 clothes. They were pretty nondescript."

"What to wear is always a big decision," said Hanna, composing herself. "Unfortunately, I can't carry clothes from every stop, so I have to pick and choose which ones to keep. I always try to have plain clothes in my backpack. Clothes that I hope won't draw attention in most places. I have a set that I've worn in a couple of different eras that'll probably work until we have a chance to obtain new ones."

Hanna turned away and slipped the cotton dress over her head. She had nothing on underneath but some panties. She reached into her backpack for a pair of jeans and a shirt. Alex stared at her nakedness with desire. After putting the clothes on, she turned to find Alex's eyes fixed on her. She blushed.

"Whoa," said Alex quietly. He turned away to change his clothes. His arousal was embarrassing.

"We have no money from 1959," said Alex, slipping on his

pants.

"Do you have any left from 1926?" asked Hanna. "It would still be good."

"That's right, I do. It's not much, but it might be enough."

He was dressed now. He dug through his backpack and came up with thirty-seven dollars.

"That'll be enough to start with," said Hanna. "We can find a thrift shop or a Salvation Army and pick up some clothes. Hotels were cheap in 1959, so we probably have enough to stay somewhere and maybe even eat something."

"How will we get to England?" asked Alex.

"One step at a time," answered Hanna. "I've found that planning too far in advance doesn't work. It closes you off from being able to make quick decisions. And sometimes quick decisions are the only way any of this works."

They left their 1863 clothes on the ground. There was no reason to pack them. Now they were ready to enter the portal.

"This time, we don't let go of each other," said Alex.

"Absolutely not," responded Hanna.

Alex took a deep breath. They interlocked their arms and held each other's hand, and then they walked through the portal.

Suddenly it was pitch black. Alex smelled the strong scent of hay. He heard a snort. A horse?

"We're in a barn," whispered Hanna. "It's night. That's good. It will allow us to sneak out of here more easily. We just have to be aware of dogs."

"You've done this before," said Alex.

"I came out onto a farm once before. It was night then, as well. Dogs began to bark almost immediately, and the farmer almost caught me. It was in the 1800s. Hopefully, this will be a bit easier."

As they crept through the barn, Hanna rubbed the heads of the horses they passed. There was a sensitivity about the gesture that impressed Alex.

They stood at the door to the barn. Across the barnyard was an older house. All the lights were off.

"It must be late," said Alex.

"Maybe. Farmers also go to bed early. But it does have the feel of the middle of the night. Let's get off the farm and find a town. Then we can focus on our next plan of action."

They took two steps outside the barn and were immediately greeted with a cacophony of barking. Three dogs were straining at ropes tied outside the farmhouse's back door.

A light went on in an upstairs room.

"We need to run," said Hanna anxiously. "We have to hope that the farmer doesn't let them go. They'll be on us in no time."

Alex spied a moving headlight in the distance.

"The road is over there," he pointed. "Maybe that's where we should go."

"Sounds good to me," she answered.

They started running, the thought of dogs catching up to them foremost in their minds.

Another light came on, this time in the kitchen. A moment later, the farmer turned on the outside light. Alex and Hanna had just reached a grove of trees that separated the farmer's property from the road.

"Anyone out here?" called the farmer. He shone a flashlight around the barnyard to ensure it wasn't a fox or a stray dog.

From their safe spot in the woods, they watched as the farmer looked around for another minute. Then he talked to the dogs and went back inside the house.

When it was safe, they started on their way. The one pair of headlights belonged to the only car on that road. The vehicle was headed in the direction of downtown Atlanta. When it was out of sight, Alex and Hanna followed. They walked along the side of the road.

They had walked almost an hour when Hanna said, "Hey. Do you realize that this is the same wagon path we were on in 1863? It was turned into a road." She stopped and looked around. "Somewhere around here, almost a hundred years ago, we encountered the soldiers."

"And yet, it was only a few hours ago," said Alex. "How strange is that? That's going to take me a long time to come to grips with. Those men lived their lives, and their children lived theirs, all in a few hours." He shook his head in wonder. "You know what else is weird? I was twenty-four in 1959. If I went back to New York, would I see myself at twenty-four?"

"You would, but one of the first things on the 'Don't List' is 'Don't try to find yourself, friends, or family members.' The repercussions of that could be devastating."

"Do they know that because it happened to someone? Or is it a theory?" asked Alex.

"I'm guessing theory," replied Hanna, "since my group is the first to travel. But it does make sense."

"Don't worry," said Alex. "I wasn't planning to. It would be a bit too creepy. Besides, my parents had disowned me by then. I wouldn't want to see them. What year were you born?"

"I was born in 2082."

Alex did some calculating. "That would be 147 years after I was born. That's a little mind-boggling. At some point, when we get some quiet time and we're not running for our lives, I want to ask you about life at the end of the 21st Century."

"And I'll ask you about life in the middle of the 20th Century," replied Hanna. "You may think that my world is beyond the scope of your imagination, and maybe it is. But your world is just as foreign to me. History books can only tell a part of the story."

"Tell me about the assassin," said Alex. "You said there are four of them?"

"That's what Tony wrote. And they are going after close to a dozen people. I'm not sure if they count Ray and Natalie as two people or lump them together as one target."

"Will we get there in time to help them?"

"Your guess is as good as mine. The assassins are human, so they have to deal with the same things we do. It depends on which portals they use to get there and when. Does the assassin arrive before Ray and Natalie? Or does he arrive after we get there? It could be anywhere in between. I'm just as much in the dark as you are. That was all the information I got from Tony. He told me how many there were and why. That's it."

"Where is your pickup and drop-off point with Tony?" asked Alex.

"It's in the Blue Ridge Mountains of Virginia," answered Hanna. "Not far from Charlottesville. Before we go to England, I want to stop off there and see if there is anything else from him."

"I assume it's well hidden?"

"Yes. I doubt if anyone could ever find the spot. It was never a well-used portal."

It was close to dawn, and they were tired. They were getting close to civilization, and the road was beginning to have traffic, so they moved into the woods. They found a secluded spot and rested against a tree. When it seemed to be the middle of the morning, judging by the sun, they continued on their way. They arrived at the outskirts of a built-up area an hour later and soon found a Salvation Army, where they bought decade-appropriate clothes. And then they stopped at a diner for breakfast. They took their time eating, enjoying the normalcy. They found a Best Western hotel a little while later and checked in as Alex and Hanna Landers. The room cost them nine dollars. Adding to what they had spent on clothes and breakfast, they still had over twenty dollars left. It would be enough for two one-way bus tickets to Charlottesville, with a little money left over.

When they reached their room, they were physically and

emotionally exhausted. They needed the day and night to rest and gather their energy. The room had two queen-sized beds, but they both knew that only one of the beds would be used. The sexual tension had been increasing by the hour.

They took turns using the shower. When Alex finished, he toweled off and opened the bathroom door, the towel tied around him. Hanna was already in one of the beds. Next to her, she had pulled down the covers. He saw her eyes appraise his body. Then she smiled. The invitation was clear.

Alex took off his towel and climbed into the bed next to her. Hanna was also naked. He touched her gently, and she returned the touch. And then months of fear for Alex and years of loneliness for Hanna disappeared as their bodies merged.

Time travel no longer existed.

Only the moment mattered.

Chapter 16

LINCOLN, NEBRASKA — 1986

"What have you determined?"

The small conference room at the Lincoln police headquarters was overflowing with bodies. The man who asked the question was the police chief. Lincoln was his city, so the woman was his responsibility. But he was also practical enough to know that his people had reached the limits of their abilities. That's why he had called the FBI, the head of the psychology department at the University of Nebraska, the head of the history department, and anyone else he could think of.

In addition to the experts, several federal government officials and scientists were present. Although this was a closed meeting, the vultures were all waiting outside. As soon as the press had caught wind of the Molly Bunker story, they had gone wild, all trying to finagle a way to interview the strange woman.

Fred Baker, the FBI psychologist, tiredly shook his head.

"I've gotta tell you. I've never seen a case like this. None of us have."

"We have a few visitors from the White House who don't yet have the full story," said the police chief. "They have the press's version, so could you bring them up to speed?"

"Sure," said Baker. "The media only has a small part of the

story. So here it is in full: Three weeks ago, a woman appeared in downtown Lincoln. She looked to be in her mid-forties and was dressed in clothing from the 1800s. Many people passed her on the street, assuming that she was either selling something or was crazy. You know how people would rather not get involved. Well, a store owner from across the street was watching her, and when he saw her start to cry, he knew he had to do something. He approached her and asked her if she was okay. He said she began to wail and said that she didn't know where she was. He immediately called the police.

"What was strange about it was her speech. The store owner said she talked like someone uneducated. Her manner of speech reminded him of various western movies he had seen. He said that the one thing he determined was that she was more scared than anyone he had ever seen."

"She was real?" asked one of the White House representatives.

"Real what?" asked Baker. "Are you asking if she was really from the old west? Of course not. But her fear was real."

"And," added the head of the history department, "she really believes she is from the old west. The scary thing is that everything she says is exactly what someone from the 1860s would believe."

"So who is she?" asked someone from the crowd.

Baker took back the reins. "She says her name is Molly Bunker and says she is thirty years old, despite looking at least ten years older."

"Which wouldn't be unusual for a woman living in the west in the 1860s," said the historian. "They led a hard life."

"She says she lives on a farm in 1866, with her husband and son," said Baker. "According to her, she was walking along the side of a stream and was getting tired. She saw a flat rock and went over to sit on it, but she found herself on the sidewalk in downtown Lincoln before she could. That's her story. We've spent three weeks talking to her and can't poke holes in any part of her story. We've had to medicate her to keep her calm, but it's not working well. She says she just wants to go home and be with her husband and son. After three weeks, we still don't know a lot."

"What *do* you know?" asked a voice from the crowd.

"I've done extensive research," said the historian, "and here's what I can tell you: The spot where she appeared was farmland in 1866. The stream she says she was walking along is exactly where Salt Creek ran and was on the outskirts of Lincoln, which was still known as the village of Lancaster at that point. I looked up her name but couldn't find any mention of her. However, I did find the name of a lawyer practicing in Lincoln in 1888. His name was Chad Bunker."

"When we asked her the names of her husband and son," said Baker, "she said both were named Chad."

That elicited some murmurs from the crowd.

"What have you determined?" asked the police chief.

"We've determined that her lack of education is real," said Baker. "She believes she is Molly Bunker from 1866. Her husband fought for the south in the Civil War...."

"And my research revealed that a Captain Chad Bunker served under General Longstreet," said the historian.

"Basically," said Baker, "we can't punch any holes in her story. Her clothes were examined and determined to be authentic from the time. So, we're stumped. The conspiracy nuts and the time travel believers are going to go wild. There is no way we can let them interview her, though. She's extremely fragile and on the verge of a total mental and emotional breakdown."

The door to the conference room burst open, and an out-of-breath uniformed police officer said, "Chief. Come quick. It's the Bunker woman!"

*****

Molly Bunker lay on the bed in tears. She hadn't stopped crying from the moment she found herself in this strange place. Men and women kept asking her questions that she couldn't answer. They didn't believe anything about her story. They said the year was 1986 and said it was 120 years from when she said it was. She didn't know math, but 120 years didn't sound right. How could she have gone 120 years? Who were these people? Where was she?

Her heart was pounding in her chest. They kept sticking needles in her arm and said it would calm her down. What would calm her down would be going home and seeing her husband and child. If she couldn't see them, she just wanted to die.

She heard a popping noise outside her room and some thumps. What was happening?

Her door opened, and a man with a black beard entered. He closed the door behind him.

"Hi Molly," he said.

She sat up.

"Who are you?"

"It doesn't matter. You know you're not supposed to be here, right?"

"I just want to go home," said Molly. The tears were flowing freely again.

"I can't send you home, but I will end this for you. What happened to you was an accident, but there is no way to fix it, I'm afraid."

He lifted a weapon and pulled the trigger. The gun popped, and a hole appeared in Molly's forehead. Blood erupted from her head, and she fell back onto the bed.

*****

"Have you found the shell?" asked the police chief.

"There isn't one," said the crime scene tech. "A bullet didn't kill Molly Bunker. I can't tell you what caused the hole. It's the same answer to your previous question. What stunned your men? I don't know. Maybe the autopsy of the woman will reveal something."

The chief looked to Baker for help. The FBI man shrugged and said, "You're not going to want to hear this, but from all appearances, Molly Bunker came from the 1860s but died from a weapon of the future. Nothing else accounts for these wounds."

"Shit!" barked the chief. "What the hell am I going to tell the press?"

Chapter 17

ATLANTA, GEORGIA—1959

Their needs were insatiable as they made love, slept, and made love several more times over the next eighteen hours. They were hungry but didn't want to leave the room searching for a place to eat. Finally, long after the sun had come up, they knew it was time to move on to the next segment of their journey. They showered together and slowly dressed, sad that their night had to end.

"How does it feel to sleep with an older man?" asked Alex after they dressed.

"You're only three years older than me," replied Hanna.

"No, I'm 147 years older. I look pretty good for my age, though, don't I?"

Hanna laughed. Over the last eighteen hours, Alex had seen her smile and laugh dozens of times. She was so different from the Hanna he had first met. They left the hotel hand in hand and went to the same coffee shop they had visited the day before. The place was empty, in its mid-morning lull.

They were in the middle of their breakfast when a shadow crossed the table. Alex assumed it was the waitress and was about to ask for more coffee when he looked up. Standing over them was the man who had tried to kill them in New York.

Alex's body froze, but his mind was immediately racing,

trying to find a way out of their situation. The man had a gun in his hand—the same strange one he had in New York.

"How did you find us?" asked Hanna. She sounded composed, but Alex knew she was anything but composed.

"Portals leave trace material. We've learned how to track it."

The man pointed the gun at Alex.

"Sorry. It's nothing personal."

At that moment, the waitress approached the man.

"Are you joining them, sir? Would you like a menu?"

The assassin was momentarily distracted, so Alex kicked out from under the table and caught the man in the knee. He dropped to the floor, and Alex kicked him again, this time in the side of the face. The waitress screamed in surprise, and the man grunted but lifted his weapon. Suddenly, there was a gunshot, and the man fell backward, blood slowly covering his chest.

Alex looked at Hanna with the smoking derringer in her hand.

"We're sorry," Hanna said to the waitress, who was sitting on the floor. "The man has been chasing us. We have no idea why."

From behind the counter, the manager looked warily at Hanna's weapon and then said, "I'll call the police. Are you folks okay?"

"We are, thank you," said Hanna. "Can I ask you to wait a minute before calling? That man and his friends have been chasing us for weeks. He's a wanted criminal. We're trying to get to Tampa. My uncle is the police chief there—Chief Matthews. We've got to get to him. It's urgent. I'll make sure he calls the Atlanta police when we arrive. So, if you can just give us a few minutes to get out of here, I'd appreciate it. We have our car out back, and we want to get on the road."

The manager looked at the waitress, who nodded. It helps to be friendly to your waitress, thought Alex.

"Okay," said the manager. "Five minutes."

"Thank you," said Alex. He reached down and picked up the man's weapon.

"Uh, should you do that?" asked the manager.

"We have to bring it to my uncle," explained Hanna. She grabbed the man's backpack, looking to make sure his Portal Finder was there, and she and Alex left through the front door. They ran down the street, turning right, then left, then right again at the intersections.

When they felt they could slow down, Alex said, "I can't believe the manager agreed to wait before calling."

"He probably didn't," said Hanna, "once he could think clearly. That's why I gave him that outlandish story about Tampa. It was just enough to confuse him. I needed him not thinking clearly."

Alex heard police sirens a few blocks away.

"And there they go. Telling him Tampa was a good idea. It might get them looking in the wrong direction and looking for us in a car."

"That's the hope."

"You really have learned to think on your feet," said Alex.

"Lots of experience," said Hanna. "Let's get to the bus station. We should buy our tickets separately and wait for others to come between us."

"Do you think we're safe from the assassins now?" asked Alex.

"I think we are," she said, "at least for the time being. But there might be a different one going after Ray and Natalie. So, they aren't safe."

They were passing a Goodwill store when a thought struck Alex.

"Sitting apart on the bus will be good, but it won't be enough," he said. "We have to make a few changes. Follow me."

Once inside, Alex headed directly to the men's clothes section and immediately found a bright red shirt.

"Perfect," he said. "Your turn."

"I get it," said Hanna. They have our descriptions, including our clothes."

"Right. They will be looking for a couple in plain clothes. Two people sitting apart, wearing bright colors, should make us almost invisible."

Hanna found an attractive green blouse.

"It brings out the green in your eyes," said Alex approvingly. "Now, one last thing."

He led Hanna over to the luggage section.

"Let's each find a small suitcase. It should be one small enough to bring with us onto the bus but shabby enough not to attract attention. We can put our backpacks in them. After all, they will be looking for two people with backpacks."

To complete the disguise, Alex found an old John Deere baseball cap. Ten minutes later, they left Goodwill, found a nearby gas station, and changed in the bathrooms.

They weren't far from the bus station, so Hanna went ahead, and Alex followed, always keeping her in sight. Once in the station, Alex looked at the board and saw that the Charlottesville bus wasn't leaving for two hours. He went into the bathroom to give some space between Hanna buying a Charlottesville ticket and him buying one. Once he had given her enough time, he bought his ticket.

It had been decided that Hanna would keep the assassin's weapon in her suitcase since she was familiar with it. Alex would keep the man's Portal Finder in his. If they somehow got separated, he could use it to find the Charlottesville portal. Hanna already knew its location. The first one there would wait for the other.

Alex looked around and found the perfect place to sit. An older lady sat by herself, eating a sandwich.

"Mind if I sit here?"

She patted the seat and said, "Please do. Would you like half of my sandwich? I won't be able to eat the whole thing."

Alex politely declined. Besides the fact that he had eaten less than an hour before, the sandwich was reeking an overpowering scent. He had little interest in finding out what was between the two pieces of bread.

Fortunately, the woman, who introduced herself as Millie, was also heading to Charlottesville, and Alex had the perfect camouflage by sitting with her on the bus. Unfortunately, once she got started, Millie talked nonstop. They got on the bus together, and Alex figured it would be a long trip.

He was wrong. The bus ride turned out to be a lot shorter than planned. They hadn't been on the road more than a half-hour when Alex felt the bus slowing down. They weren't near a town, so something must be wrong. Then he saw the flashing lights of several cars.

The police!

Chapter 18

Alex looked back at Hanna as casually as possible. Her face wasn't displaying any emotions.

"What do you suppose it is?" asked Millie.

"Maybe you forgot to buy your ticket," said Alex with a laugh. Meanwhile, his heart was thudding in his chest.

The doors opened, and three Georgia State Police officers climbed aboard.

"We're sorry to disturb everyone," said the one in charge. "We should only be a few minutes."

They started down the aisle. When they reached a man in his thirties, they asked him for some I.D. Satisfied, they moved on to the next person of interest. Then they reached Alex.

"May we see some I.D.?

Alex pretended to reach into his back pocket when Millie grabbed his arm and stopped him.

"You don't need to see his identification. He's with me."

The officer's eyes lit up.

"Millie. How are you? Heading up to see your sister?"

"I am, Frank. Who are you looking for?"

"A man and a woman in their thirties who shot and killed someone in the Hilltop Diner. The workers say it was self-defense, but they left the scene, and we need to talk to them. They told people they were going to Tampa by car, but we don't think that's true, so we're checking all the buses."

"I hope you find them, but if it was self-defense, I hope you'll go easy on them."

"We'll see. Say hi to your sister for me."

"I will."

The officers moved on. Alex was holding his breath.

"May I see some identification?"

Alex heard Hanna say, "I'm afraid I don't have any. I was boating yesterday, and my purse fell overboard. I'm heading home to Charlottesville so I can replace my license."

"Well, ma'am, I'm afraid you're going to have to come with us. You fit the description of the woman involved."

"But that's ridiculous. I heard you say that it's a couple. I'm traveling alone."

"I'm sorry, Ma'am. If we turn out to be wrong, we will get you on the next bus to Charlottesville."

Alex glanced back at her, figuring that it would appear odd if he didn't. Hanna didn't look his way and was escorted off the bus. Her suitcase was still in the bin above her seat.

The police checked the I.D. of one more man then left with Hanna in tow.

Frank came back in and approached Millie.

"I'm sorry, Millie, but I have to ask. How well do you know this man? He fits the profile of the man we're looking for."

"I understand," she replied. "This is Alex. He's the son of an old friend. He's heading home to visit his mom. He stayed the night at my house and has been with me all day."

Frank thought about it for a second, then said, "Okay. Just checking. Have a great day, Millie."

Alex felt sick. How was he going to free Hanna? The bus started to move. Alex knew he had to get off at the next stop. Somehow, he would have to get Hanna's suitcase without drawing suspicion.

"That's okay," Millie whispered. "Just think it out. Don't panic."

Alex stiffened. "What do you mean?"

"Your woman will be fine."

"I...I don't know what you're talking about."

Millie looked at him with a twinkle in her eyes.

"I may look like a simple old lady who talks too much, but I notice things. I worked for forty years at the Atlanta police station switchboard. I've seen everything. I saw how you looked at her at the bus station. I thought at first that maybe you were just flirting, but it was more than that."

"How did you know? I didn't even look at her."

"You don't *think* you looked at her. But, in reality, you couldn't keep your eyes off her. And she couldn't keep hers off you."

"Wow. I didn't know that." He touched her gently on the arm. "Why did you lie for me just now?"

"It looked like you needed help. So, who are you really?" Millie asked. "And don't worry. I have a plan to help you. I know every police officer in this half of the state. But we can't do anything until the next stop."

"Okay." Alex thought about how much he wanted to say. "My name really is Alex, and a few months ago, I was a history teacher in New York City. And then my life turned upside down. I can't tell you how because you'd never believe me. You'd think I belonged in a loony bin, but I don't. It's all real. In the process, I met Hanna. Actually, she saved my life from the man who later tried to kill us in Atlanta."

"Why was he trying to kill you?"

"I can't tell you that. I would love to tell you, but...."

"But I would think you belonged in a loony bin."

"Right."

"Well, I'll tell you what. I'll help you, but I want something in return. We'll be at our next stop in about half an hour. But, before we get there, I want to hear your story. As crazy as I might think you are after hearing it, I will still help you. So, you have a few minutes to decide whether you want to help your woman get out of jail."

Alex couldn't help but smile. Millie was an iron-willed old lady. She wasn't making the ultimatum to be mean. She had a genuine interest in his story and wanted to add it to the vast collection of stories she must have heard in her years at the police station. But he couldn't tell her.

"Millie, you have to understand. It's not that I don't want to tell you. Hell, I want to tell everybody. But I can't. It's too dangerous to the world and the future. If I tell you, and then you tell another person, and that person tells others, it could have serious ramifications for the future. So, I just can't do it."

He looked around. The seats around them were empty, so hopefully, no one had heard their conversation.

"Let me ask you something," said Millie, glaring at Alex. "In all the yapping I've been doing since we met, have I said anything about other people? Have I said anything that shouldn't have been said? An obvious secret? No. Alex, I know how to keep a secret. I saw and heard things at the police station that can never be repeated. If they were, it would harm a lot of good people. Mistakes are made, secrets are discovered, and a person's life can be destroyed in a second. I am liked and trusted by hundreds of police officers because they know that anything I hear or see that I shouldn't, will never be revealed. 'Ramifications for the future.' That's an interesting comment."

Alex could tell Millie the story, but what would Hanna say when he told her? He was more worried about her reaction than he was about revealing the secret. What if she felt she could no longer trust him? That would be the worst thing that could ever happen to him. His feelings toward Hanna were sitting deep in his soul. He knew now that he was in love with her, and he couldn't jeopardize that. And there was no way he could tell Millie and not tell Hanna that he had revealed the secret.

"Alex?"

He suddenly realized she had been trying to get his attention.

"I'm sorry," he said. "I was deep in thought."

"I'll still help you," she said, squeezing his arm. "You don't have to worry. That was unfair of me to pressure you. I can respect someone who keeps a secret. Just understand, I'm eighty-two years old. I don't have much longer to live."

"Do you have cancer or something?"

"No, nothing like that. I'm just old. I have a weak heart. I have arthritis. I have many medical issues and don't have much longer in this world. So, to hear a good story—especially an unbelievable one—would make my day."

"This one would more than make your day," said Alex. "But I still can't tell you without talking to Hanna first. This is as much her story as it is mine, and it would be unfair of me to share it without her."

"That's one of the most sensitive things I've ever heard," said Millie.

She didn't say anything else, and Alex wasn't sure if he should say something, so he elected to remain silent.

The bus pulled into the next stop, and Alex and Millie stood up.

"Sonny, could you get me my other bag from that bin over there?" said Millie in a loud voice, pointing to where Hanna's bag was.

"I'd be happy to," replied Alex. He retrieved Hanna's bag, then grabbed Millie's bag and his own and followed Millie off the bus.

"Change of plans," Millie said to the driver. "I'm getting out here."

"How are you going to get to Charlottesville?" asked Alex when they reached the platform.

"There's another bus in a few hours," she answered. "Don't worry about me. I need to use the phone."

They found the pay phone, and Millie inserted money.

"Rhonda? This is Millie Halpern. I'm good. How are you? Has Frank from the state police arrived? He has? Could I talk to him? It's important."

She waited while Rhonda found Frank. Finally, he got on the phone.

"Frank? It's Millie. I saw your young couple. They were here at the Braselton bus station. I'm positive it was them. They saw me looking at them from the bus window, and they ran. It's like they knew they were recognized. I think you have the wrong woman. Oh, okay. Can you bring her up when you come? She left a bag on the bus, and I have it here. I'm at the bus station. Okay, I'll see you in about an hour."

She hung up and faced Alex. "Done. They already realized that they had the wrong woman. They are heading up this way and are bringing her with them."

Alex hugged Millie.

"Thank you. You have no idea how much I appreciate all that you did."

"Maybe Hanna will agree to tell me your story."

The police showed up a little later with Hanna, who walked warily toward Alex and Millie.

"I retrieved your bag, young lady," said Millie.

"Thank you so much," replied Hanna.

Millie described to Frank the fictitious couple she had seen, and the police set off in pursuit.

Alex hugged Hanna.

"This is Millie. She knew immediately that we were a couple and that we were the couple the police were looking for."

"Thank you," said Hanna. "I don't know why you did it, but you saved our lives."

"I did it for the story," answered Millie, "and because I like Alex."

"What story?"

"Your story. I know it's a whopper, but Alex refused to tell me. He said he couldn't tell me without you here."

Alex faced Hanna. "I think she deserves to know. We owe her. I'm convinced that she'll keep it to herself."

Hanna thought for a minute and then said to Millie, "There was a time when I would have said that there was no way I would tell you anything about our story, but I'm indebted to you. And frankly, I just don't care anymore. I'm tired." She reached out and took Alex's hand.

"I don't mind telling Millie," she said to him, "That was a nice thing she did for us. But no future events. Just our story. Nothing that could affect time."

Millie cocked her head. "That's twice that the future has been referred to. If that means what I think it means, you have my attention. Let's get something to eat. My treat."

They found a diner and sat in a corner booth, away from others. After they ordered, Millie looked at Alex with anticipation.

"You start," said Hanna, touching his hand.

"I told you that I was a teacher in New York and that my life changed suddenly," said Alex. "It changed because I was a teacher in New York in 1973."

There was a momentary silence as he let that sink in.

"I had a feeling it was going to be something like that," said Millie. "As much as you are trying to blend in, you two are definitely not from here—I'm talking both place and time." She addressed Hanna. "Are you from 1973, as well? My guess is no."

"You are very perceptive," said Hanna. "No, I'm from the year 2105."

"I see."

"You either don't seem surprised," said Alex, "or you already don't believe us."

"Oddly enough, I might believe you. Go on."

"I was on my way to my job at a local school," began Alex, "when I saw one of my students go into an abandoned building. So, I followed...."

*****

Two hours and many cups of coffee later, they finished their story.

"Do you know why I believe you?" asked Millie. "It's because you two told the story seamlessly. You went back and forth between you without skipping a beat. You couldn't do that even if you memorized the story. Not that I necessarily need it, but do you have any kind of proof?"

Hanna reached into her bag and showed Millie the Portal Finder below table level so that no one else could see it. She turned it on so that all the lights were blinking, and a map came up on the screen. Millie was mesmerized.

"This is how we find the time portals," Hanna said.

Then she pulled out the weapon that the assassin used.

"And this weapon shoots energy charges, not bullets. You can adjust it to kill or to stun."

"That's interesting," said Alex. "Like the phasers on the Star Trek TV show."

"Right," said Hanna. "Even I've heard of Star Trek. I even saw one of the movies."

"There were movies?"

"And several different series. I watched a lot of very old TV series and movies in preparation for my job."

"What are you talking about?" asked Millie.

"Something from the future," said Alex. "So, you've heard our story. Do you think we are mental cases?"

"I don't," answered Millie. "The story was believable, but the gadgets were the final proof."

"And you won't tell anyone?" asked Hanna.

"I won't." She hesitated. "Where are you going now?"

"We have to stop someplace outside Charlottesville, and then we have to get to England somehow so that we can warn the two travelers there."

"And then more traveling in time?"

Hanna looked at Alex. "I don't know. Probably."

"Then I have a request."

Alex could feel it coming.

"Please take me with you."

Chapter 19

"Impossible," said Hanna, shaking her head. "The Time Travel Project is shutting down for a reason. It's too dangerous for the world. That's why the assassins are here, to eliminate everyone who has traveled who is still alive. The minute you go through a portal, you will register with their computers, and you'll be on their radar."

"I have no idea what you are talking about."

"I think the word 'computer' is probably throwing her," said Alex with a chuckle.

"Okay, I'll put it simply. You might be killed."

"Do I look worried? Hanna, I'm eighty-two years old and in bad physical condition. How much longer do you think I'll live?"

"And what if we decide to stay in England and not do any more time travel?" asked Alex.

"Then I'll either stay there or come back here. You have nothing to lose, and neither do I."

"Has anyone ever told you that you're a pain in the neck?" asked Alex.

"Just about every day for the past eighty-two years."

Alex and Hanna looked at each other and sighed.

"I have a question for you," said Millie. "How are you getting to England?"

"I try not to think too far in advance," said Hanna.

"If you had a passport, it might make your options easier."

"I have one," said Hanna, laughing, "but it's from 1992."

"I know someone who can make you a couple of passports. You won't find any better fake ones."

"I'm confused," said Alex.

"Because I seem like a sweet old lady?" asked Millie. "How does a sweet old lady know a forger? I may be old, but I'm not always as sweet as I seem. And I wasn't always old. I might not have been a cop, but I worked around honest cops, crooked cops, and criminals. I learned some things from all three, and I got to know many people on both sides of the law. I found out something over the years. The honest ones aren't always good, and the crooked ones aren't always bad. There's a gray area there. The forger I know just happens to be a really nice guy."

"We don't have any money to pay for them," said Hanna.

"Don't worry about it," answered Millie. "He owes me a big favor. Besides, I have a lot of money. It's that 'gray area' thing. Don't ask."

"Can you give us a moment?" asked Hanna.

"Of course. I'll go use the bathroom."

"So?" asked Alex when Millie left.

"This goes against everything I was trained for," answered Hanna. "I've spent twelve years being so careful about what I say to people, who I associate with, and the decisions I make. I'm having a little trouble accepting it. On the other hand, I never counted on assassins coming through time to kill me."

"So the rules go out the window," said Alex.

"Some of them, maybe. We still have to be extra careful. We still have a responsibility to the world. The last thing we want to do is create a situation where time gets affected. In other words, we still have to be diligent, even though we are being hunted. What do you think about Millie?"

"I've only known her a few hours, but I think I've got a pretty good picture of her, and I think we should include her," said Alex, "but not if you have reservations. When it comes to time travel decisions, I will always defer to you."

"You won't always have to," said Hanna. "You're picking it up pretty fast. As for Millie, we need her help with the passports and the money. It might cramp our style if you know what I mean."

"I know. I've already thought of that." He reached over and took her hand and kissed it. "But she does have a lot of common sense, and she's street smart. So I'm not sure she would hold us back unless we have to move quickly."

"What's the worst that can happen?" asked Hanna. "We take her with us to England. If we decide to use a portal and determine that she's a liability, we ditch her before going to the portal. She can always fly back to America with no harm done. We just have to make sure we don't ever reveal the location of any outgoing portals."

At Alex's questioning look, Hanna said, "I saw your reaction when I said the word 'ditch.' There have been times over the last twelve years when I've had to be cold and callous. I'm sure I've hurt people. But, unfortunately, it can be a cold and uncaring business when it comes to keeping all this secret. It's the part I've hated the most. So, I'm okay about including her, but I have to warn you that there may come a time when we will have to jettison her—and I'm using the cold term purposely—and you have to be ready to accept that."

"I get it," replied Alex. "I really do. I've already had to lie a lot in the past couple of months. This just takes it to the next level."

They saw Millie leaving the bathroom.

"Oh, and by the way," said Hanna, suddenly regaining her smile, "you said that Millie was confused by the computer reference. If you had any idea what they began doing with computers not too long after your time in 1973, you'd be confused, too."

"Hey, I'm already confused," Alex said with a laugh.

Millie sat down at the table and said, "Can I take it from your smiles that I'm in?"

"Yes," replied Hanna, "as long as you understand how important it is to keep all of this secret. One loose word or action could be devastating to the future of this world. We know that you've taken on a lot of responsibility over the years, but this responsibility far surpasses any of that."

"I understand. I really do. I also know that deep down, there is something dangerous about you, Hanna. You're not afraid to do what you have to do. You take this seriously, and you will expect that I take it seriously, or else. I can respect that. In fact, I respect it so much that I have to come clean."

Alex's eyebrows shot up.

"I am eighty-two, but I'm not sick. I don't have a heart condition. I have no plans to die anytime soon. I said I was dying so that you would feel safe in taking me along with you. Then, if you had to make a hard decision, you wouldn't feel bad about getting rid of me. I know now that my health wouldn't play a part in your decision. So, I want you to know that my health is fine, and I can keep up with you."

Hanna was silent for a minute. Alex was also quiet as he waited to see what she said.

Finally, Hanna responded, picking her words carefully.

"Millie, I appreciate your honesty, but here's the thing: I've spent the last twelve years not trusting anyone. When Alex and I met, I knew that I had found someone I could trust completely. I felt relaxed for the first time. To include you took a lot of inner compromise on my part. The fact is, we need your help with the passports and the money. In that sense, it's a business deal. But even in a business deal, trust has to be first and foremost. I accept what you're saying, but if you lie again, we will jettison you immediately, no matter where we are. Is that clear?"

"Perfectly clear. You'll never have to worry about it happening again."

"Then let's go to England," said Hanna.

Chapter 20

CAPE COD, MASSACHUSETTS—1933

"Holy crap! I've gone back in time."

That was what Brad Oppenheim thought the moment he discovered himself in 1933 Cape Cod, and not 1999 Cape Cod, and realized what had happened. It was so exciting!

He had come to the Cape to attend a regional science fiction convention in Hyannis. After an evening of a little too much drink at his hotel with some fellow conventioneers, Brad decided to go for a walk on the beach. Unfortunately, his impaired judgment and vision caused him to veer off the beach and walk into a large bush before reaching the beach.

Suddenly it was light—daytime. Had he passed out and just woken up? He didn't remember passing out. And he was still standing. You don't pass out standing up.

He looked around. Something was different. Where was the hotel? There were a few people on the beach. What the hell kind of swimsuits were they wearing? A nearby road was surprisingly empty, with only a few cars passing by. Was there some kind of antique car show going on?

Then it hit him. Could it be? Had he really gone back in time? He had come to Cape Cod for a science fiction convention. How ironic was that?

Two young men walked by on the beach in swimsuits—sleeveless tops and short bottoms—they looked like they were straight out of a photograph.

"Excuse me," said Brad. "This may sound like a strange question, but what year is it?"

The men looked at him strangely, staring at his jeans and Star Wars t-shirt. Then they laughed and walked off. A few minutes later, an older man came by in attire similar to the younger men. Brad repeated his question. This time, after staring at him for a full ten seconds, the man replied, "1933."

He had done it! He didn't know how he did it, but he had gone back in time. He didn't have a camera on him. That was too bad. He needed some proof to take back to his friends. Maybe he could find an object to take back as proof. How would he get it? He had no money that would be accepted here. Maybe they wouldn't notice the difference if he gave a dollar bill. Forget that. He could just bring his friends here. Yeah, that's what he'd do.

Brad returned to the bush and walked into it. He looked around and saw a couple of women watching him.

Nope. Still in 1933. Maybe he had to go in the opposite side. Again, he went into the bush. Again, it didn't work. Meanwhile, the two women were laughing at his strange antics.

Suddenly, Brad began to panic. What if he couldn't get back? What if he was stuck here? He had no money, and he was dressed strangely for the time.

He ran into the bush from all angles, but other than scratching himself, nothing happened.

The women on the beach had stopped laughing and now were looking at him with concern. A few other bathers had joined them.

One of the men called out, "Hey, buddy. Are you okay?"

Brad was so distraught he couldn't answer. He ran up toward the road but stopped when he heard his name called. Who knew his name?

"Brad. Brad Oppenheim. I'm over here."

A man was standing next to a building and was beckoning to him. Brad had no choice but to see what the man wanted. He had to be from the future if he knew Brad's name. Maybe it was his ticket home.

"You know who I am," said Brad as he approached the man. He was a big man with a black beard.

"I do. You're not supposed to be here."

"I know that. Can you get me home?"

"I'm sorry, but I can't."

"Why not?"

"There is no way to get back to where you started. It doesn't work that way."

"Why not?"

"It just doesn't."

"Then how do I get home?"

"I'm afraid you don't."

The man pulled a weapon from a bag and pointed it at Brad.

"No!" Brad screamed.

A moment later, Brad was lying dead on the ground. The assassin removed all of Brad's clothes and threw them in his bag.

Brad's naked body was discovered later that day.

He was never identified.

Chapter 21

CHARLOTTESVILLE, VIRGINIA—1959

Millie proved to be true to her word.

The three of them hopped on the next bus to Charlottesville. Millie took Alex and Hanna to her sister's house, where they were given the guest room. Millie's sister, Agnes, was a simple woman a few years older than Millie. She made them a dinner of meatloaf and mashed potatoes. She asked no questions about Alex and Hanna, and after dinner, she excused herself and went to bed. The other three sat in the small living room with coffee and homemade cookies.

"Your sister is nice," said Alex.

"That's kind of you, but as you can see, she's not quite right. She's only a shell of her former self. She's never been a curious or adventurous person. She became a librarian and lived a solitary life. She's a good person, but she never had any interest in anything more from life. Now she is going senile."

"Doesn't she need you to help her?" asked Alex.

"She developed a few close friends over the years. They live in town and are good to her. They take turns stopping by every couple of days. They've become more like family to her than I am. She's closer to them than she is to me and has been for a lot of years."

"Don't you worry about her missing you when you're gone?" asked Hanna.

"I only see her every couple of months, and to be honest, a year from now, she won't remember me at all. So no, the timing is good."

They said goodnight and went to their rooms. Alex and Hanna picked up where they left off the night before and spent hours making love, finally giving in to exhaustion around three a.m.

When Alex questioned about her sexual energy, Hanna said, "I'm catching up on twelve years of abstinence."

"Works for me," he replied.

Millie left early the following day to find her forger friend. She returned around noon and announced an afternoon appointment for pictures.

"The passports will only take a day, so I think we can be ready to leave in a couple of days."

"Thank you, Millie," said Hanna. "I know I was kind of hard on you, but I want you to know how much I appreciate your help."

"Not a problem," replied Millie. "I appreciate strong women, and you're a strong one."

They met with the forger that day. He was a nervous little man who owned a camera store and didn't want his name revealed, even though his name was on the store's sign. He promised the passports the next day.

When Alex saw them the following day, he compared them to Millie's passport and thought they looked official. They left the next morning.

Millie told Agnes that she was going to England for a vacation. Alex saw tears in Millie's eyes when she embraced her sister.

"To England by way of Washington DC?" she asked after

saying goodbye to her sister.

"Not yet," replied Hanna. "We have to make a side trip. We need a car."

"Do you have a driver's license?" Alex asked Millie.

"I do, but I never drive anymore."

"That's okay. We just need it to rent a car. I can drive, but you need to rent it."

They called for a taxi to take them to the nearest rental agency. Less than an hour later, with Alex driving, they were on their way out of town in a Ford Thunderbird.

"Always wanted to drive one of these," said Alex.

"Boys and toys," said Hanna.

"Do boys still have toys where you come from?" asked Alex.

"They do. The toys are very different, but the childish behavior is the same."

"Hopefully, I won't get pulled over," said Alex. "I don't have a license."

"We have the means to deal with that now," said Hanna. She pulled out the assassin's gun from her backpack.

"Wait a minute! You'd shoot him?" asked Millie incredulously.

"I'd stun him. Don't worry, it wouldn't hurt him. It would just disable him for a while."

"I guess I have a lot to learn," said Millie.

"We all do," said Alex. "And we'll get back to that 'childish behavior' comment later."

The road they took was winding and steep as they entered the Blue Ridge. Alex kept glancing down at the Portal Finder in Hanna's lap, and Millie leaned over the front seat to watch it.

"Hey guys," Hanna finally said, "I'll let you know when we're close."

"Sorry. I've just never seen anything like it," said Millie. "Is everything from your time like this?"

"Too much of it is," replied Hanna with a frown. "You don't know how lucky you are not to have all the technology that overpowers our lives."

"I'm amazed at all of our technology in 1973," said Alex. "I can't imagine what it's like in 2105."

"I'm afraid that 1973 was still in the dark ages," said Hanna. "It was in the years after that when technology really took off. Even if you moved forward only twenty-five years from 1973, you'd be amazed at the changes. It would all be foreign to you. Technology just developed faster and faster after that. By my lifetime, it had reached a point where scientists and technology experts were actually trying to scale back. In my opinion, it was too late."

"I don't think I would like your world," said Millie.

"No, you wouldn't. I don't even like it," Hanna said quietly.

Millie heard her and asked, "Do you want to go home?"

"No. To be honest, I don't know where I want to go." She looked at Alex and said, "But for the first time in my life, I know who I want to be with."

Alex reached over and took her hand. Millie, sensing the mood of the moment, sat back in her seat.

"We're getting close," announced Hanna. "Somewhere soon, you're going to have to find a place to pull over."

A minute later, Alex saw a path between some trees. It might have even once been used as a road. Maybe by hunters? He slowed down and pulled in. He went as far as he could so the car would be hidden from the main road, and then he parked behind a grove of trees.

"Perfect," said Hanna. "We'll have to do a little walking, but it's not too far." She turned to Millie. "Would you rather come or stay here?"

"Hey, I'm all in. A little walking won't stop me."

The trip took longer than expected, as it was all uphill. The trees thinned out, and a rocky terrain took over. They stopped to rest several times, mainly for Millie's sake.

At one of the rest stops, Millie asked, "So let me get this straight. Your friend on the other end of the portal puts material in the portal, and it suddenly appears here?"

"Right," said Hanna.

"And if you want to leave something for him, you put it in the portal?"

"Not *in* the portal. Tony would end up here when he tried to retrieve it if we did that. So we leave it in a spot outside the portal. It's a designated spot, and he'll look for it there."

Alex did some figuring in his head and then said, "So if you leave something for him, it will sit here for something like 155 years? What if someone finds it?"

"We try to find locations that are out of the way. We just have to hope that no one finds it. Tony sends it in a sealed container that looks like its environment. I will take out anything he left for me and replace it with anything I want him to see."

"And even though it sits there for 155 years, items don't pile up?" asked Alex.

"It's one of the aspects to this we don't quite understand yet. When I take something that he leaves or vice versa, it disappears. Somehow, it's synchronous. That's the only word I can think of to explain it."

"So it doesn't really sit for 155 years?" asked Alex.

"It does, but it doesn't. Remember, we no longer exist in Tony's world. So the moment I put something in the secret location, it's already there in 2105. Actually, it's now probably 2117, his time. Twelve years have passed since the travelers left. Anyway, when Tony puts something in the portal, it appears here instantly."

"Whoa, I think I'm getting a headache," said Millie.

"You and me both," said Alex.

Hanna laughed.

"Isn't this a regular drop-off point?" asked Alex.

"One of them. Not knowing exactly where I'll be, sometimes he leaves the same material in two or three spots, just to make sure I get it."

"Then why do you need the Portal Finder to locate it?"

"You mean to say that you wouldn't get lost around here?" asked Hanna. "I could come here a hundred times and still need the Portal Finder to find the exact place."

"Good point."

When they reached the spot, Hanna spied the box almost immediately. The portal was between two large boulders, and the container was in the middle of the spot. Hanna opened it and pulled out a note.

"This doesn't bode well," she said. "He usually leaves more than this."

She read the note aloud:

Hanna, they are on to me. I'm running for my life. This will probably be the last correspondence I can send you. They know that you killed one of their assassins, so they are sending a replacement. They might even send more than one. I can no longer get any information. You are all in danger. I gave you a list of the people stuck in time and targeted by the assassins. You can cross off Molly Bunker and Brad Oppenheim. They've been eliminated.

I'm debating using a portal myself to get away from the people after me. I'd still have to deal with the assassins, though. I don't know what to do. If I come through, I'll try to find you.

Take care and good luck!

Tony

p.s. Simone is alive! I don't know where she is, but they've been tracking her.

"Who's Simone?" asked Alex.

"She's the sixth traveler, the one we lost contact with. She became a good friend. I hope she's okay."

"What did the rest of his message mean?" asked Millie.

"It meant that the man we shot in Atlanta has been replaced. Unfortunately, that means there are still four—or maybe more—assassins out there."

She looked at Alex with fear in her eyes.

"And we have no idea what they look like."

Chapter 22

"Millie," said Alex, "it's not too late to bow out. You haven't gone through a portal, so they can't track you."

"Nope. You can't get rid of me that easily. So let me say for the hundredth time: I'm eighty-two. What have I got to lose? But you have my permission to jettison—that was the word you used, right?"

Hanna nodded.

"You have the right to jettison me at any time if you think I'm holding you back."

With that settled, they made their way back to the car. There was no need for Hanna to leave Tony a note. She had a feeling that he'd never return to the portal.

They drove to Washington and found a flight at Washington National Airport to London that evening. Their new forged passports passed inspection, and the flight proved to be uneventful.

Millie had taken out a good bit of money from the bank, and when they landed, she exchanged a lot of it for British currency. Hanna and Alex had both been to London in their lives, but Millie hadn't. So, while they couldn't spend the time sightseeing, they found a cab and asked the driver to take them the long way to Liverpool Street Station so that Millie could see some sights. When they arrived at the train station, Millie hugged them both and thanked them for taking the time to do that.

Hanna had already used the Portal Finder to find out where they were going, and they caught a train to the town of Saxmundham.

"So, you can only go in one direction using these portals?" asked Millie when they were on their way. They had a compartment to themselves.

"That's right," answered Hanna. "That's why it's such a convoluted system to try to get anywhere specific. You might have to access ten or fifteen portals to arrive at your intended destination. The Saxmundham portal is one-way to 1958 or so from the future."

"And you have to access it from the future?" asked Alex. "You can't go through it in 1935 and arrive there?"

"No," said Hanna. "Portals can go ahead in time or back in time, but they can only do one or the other. In this case, 1958 is the destination, but you can only get there from the future. And to make it more complicated, it has to be a certain number of years in the future. In other words, you couldn't access the portal in, say, 1960 or 61. It's too close. It might not be until 1970 that the portal appears. It's not an exact science, and the time frame can vary with each portal."

"But there are portals that can go ahead in time, right?" asked Millie.

"Considering we arrived in 1959 from 1863, I can answer that question from experience," said Alex.

Alex and Hanna took turns dozing, but Millie was transfixed by the scenery and couldn't sleep.

At one point, Alex opened his eyes and saw the smile on Millie's face and felt that they had made the right decision allowing her to come.

That evening, they arrived in Saxmundham, and Hanna again used the Portal Finder. It led them to a house off the main street.

Lights were on inside.

"Well, someone is home," said Alex. "Let's hope it's them."

"What's their story?" asked Millie.

"I don't know much of it," answered Hanna. "Natalie O'Brien was a famous movie actress who accidentally went through a portal in 2009 in Hollow Rock, Arizona, which led her to 1870. Ray Burton found out about it in 2021 and somehow contacted her. He then went through the portal, in part to help her and in part to find someone else who had also gone through. I'm sure we'll get the full story when we meet them."

"How long have they been here?" asked Millie.

"About a year, assuming the portal deposited them in 1958."

That seemed to be the end of the questions, so Hanna asked, "Is everyone ready?"

"Yes."

"Yes."

"Then let's do it."

Hanna knocked on the door.

PART TWO

Chapter 23

SOUTHEND, ENGLAND—SUMMER 1959

It was a beautiful summer's day. Of course, we had found that any day it wasn't raining in England could be considered beautiful. But this had been a legitimately gorgeous weekend by the sea.

Natalie and I were walking the Southend Pier. She had stopped at a booth that sold funny postcards and was reading them to me. Looking at her laughing, I was filled with warmth. The difference between this Natalie and the Natalie I first met was night and day.

When I first made contact with her, Natalie was scared and confused. She had been in Hollow Rock, Arizona, 1870 for several months. Luckily, there were already a couple of travelers from the future who could explain things to her. But, while it calmed her down, it couldn't help the loneliness that she felt.

Through a series of events, I found out that she was there, and I was able to make contact with her. By then, all the people she had become friendly with had either left or were dead, and I promised my help. While I never specifically said that I would come through the portal to help her in person, deep down, I knew I would. Ray Burton, tough former war correspondent, was going back to rescue his damsel in distress.

Yeah, well, Natalie turned out to be a lot tougher than my

male ego was expecting, and she became as much my savior as I was hers. In the process, we fell in love, even though at fifty, I was almost twenty years older than her. That didn't seem to matter to Natalie.

We had been in Saxmundham for almost a year and a half, living as Ray and Natalie Bean. Natalie worked at a local pub and had hit it off with all the locals. I was the lesser involved half of the couple. People knew me as the writer who holed up in the house every day. That wasn't exactly true. We went out a lot together, and they did know me. They just knew and liked Natalie better.

This was our first vacation away from Saxmundham since we had arrived, and we were having the time of our lives. We had gone to the seaside village of Southend—south of us and east of London—which had become quite a vacation spot for English families. It had a mile-and-a-half-long pier filled with shops and attractions. I had once written an article about Southend, and I remembered that in October 1959, the end of the pier would catch fire, and about 300 people would have to climb onto boats to make it back to shore. I didn't remember reading that anyone died, and I had received good instruction from time travelers like "Uncle Jim," Alan Garland, and others not to talk about future events. So, the news of the fire that would happen in a couple of months had to remain with me.

We grabbed some fish and chips and sat at a table by the railing overlooking the water below. Natalie had gone into reflection mode and was staring into space.

"I was thinking that I'm ready to go home if we could somehow get there."

"You're not happy here?" I asked.

"Are you?"

"I'm happy with you. I don't care where that is. But I know what you're saying. It's been nice to experience the sedate life of a small English town, but I think you and I need more than that."

"It's strange to live in a place and time where we know the future. I don't think I like knowing the future," she said.

"Funny that you say that. I don't either. Especially as we are about to hit the 1960s. We'll be faced with Vietnam, assassinations, riots, and more. I'm not sure I want to experience all that firsthand. So we'd have to find a portal that could get us past 2021 when I left. It was explained to me that it would be a disaster of massive proportions for me to arrive before I left. You could arrive any time after 2009, but I have to arrive after 2021."

"And if I arrive between 2009 and 2021, we wouldn't have met yet. It's way too confusing, so after 2021 is fine with me," said Natalie. She laid her hand on mine and looked me in the eyes. "The truth. Do you think we will make it home?"

"The truth is that I don't know," I responded. "They all warned me that getting home could be problematic at best and impossible at worst."

"And yet, you still came through the portal to try to take me home."

"No matter what happens, it was still the best decision I've ever made."

I knew I'd get a kiss for that, and she didn't disappoint.

The problem, of course, was where we wanted to go if we couldn't make it home. When we landed in Saxmundham, we were so taken by its old-English quaintness we thought we wanted to stay. It was a romantic thought, but it eventually became old. Maybe it was because we could see the future, as Natalie said. And perhaps it was something different. These people lived simple lives. Truth be told—and maybe it was an unfair judgment because it was a different time—their lives were frustratingly simple. The men woke up, went to work, came home to a nice dinner made by the wife, then the men would head over to the pub for the evening. I had no idea what the wives' lives were like. The whole thing lacked substance.

Maybe an argument could be made that life in the 21st Century lacked substance, but it was the life I knew. So, if I made judgments, that was why.

Which didn't solve the problem of where we would go if we couldn't make it home. That meant that if we were serious about finding a way home, we had to dedicate ourselves to that. We'd have to keep trying portals until we found the one that could take us back.

There was another problem. The NSA had been after me when I left. Would they still be after me when I got back? Probably. Did that put Natalie's life in danger? Probably.

I decided not to think about it for the rest of the vacation.

✶✶✶✶✶

We'd been home a week and had fallen back into our groove, with me continuing my book about our adventures and Natalie working at the pub. Now that we had decided to leave England, she enjoyed her work again. She had always liked the people. It was the thought of staying there forever that had put a damper on everything. Now she could enjoy the people again, as we planned our next step.

It was late afternoon, and I anticipated Natalie's return from work in a few minutes. Even though I had lots to do in my book, I always missed Natalie when she was at work and couldn't wait for her to return.

I heard a sound coming from the basement. An animal? Animals would often come through the portal. I'd have to catch them and set them free outside. So, I didn't give it much thought as I approached the basement door. But just to be safe, I retrieved the Glock that I had brought with me through time and put it behind my back in my belt.

I opened the basement door and was surprised to find a tall, middle-aged man standing there. He had sandy hair and the trace of a mustache. We had never had a person come through the portal in all the time we'd been there.

I took a step back in surprise.

"Can I help you?" I asked. I had my hand on my gun behind my back

"Ray Burton?"

"Yes.... Uh, no. I'm Ray Bean."

"You're not supposed to be here."

"I'm sorry?"

"You are not supposed to be here. Where is Natalie O'Brien?"

This didn't bode well.

"I don't know a Natalie O'Brien. And what do you mean that I'm not supposed to be here?"

"You came through time, so you must be eliminated."

He pulled out a weapon of some sort and pointed it at me. I jumped out of the way just as he shot. It made a strange sound, kind of like the pop of a Nerf gun, and something hot creased my ribs and ripped my shirt.

I tried to kick him in the groin but missed and got his hip. He went down onto one knee, so I kicked him in the face. His weapon went flying, and he dove at me and drove me to the floor. I flipped him over my head, and he landed with a thud on the floor but was immediately up again and attacked me. We went down in a heap. I started pounding on his head, but he landed a shot to the solar plexus, and I fell away from him, unable to breathe. I kicked out but landed a harmless blow on his shoulder. He sat on my chest and punched me hard in the face, and my head bounced off the floor. Everything swirled in front of my eyes.

The man reached over and grabbed his weapon, then stood up and pointed it at me. Everything was still swirling around me.

"Just doing my job," he said.

And then I heard a crack, and the man fell on top of me. He landed with his face right in front of mine. I could tell from his eyes that he was dead.

"Ray, are you okay?" It was Natalie.

"I think I'll live if the world stops swirling around me. You came in the nick of time."

"I arrived and could hear the noise from outside. I saw him hit you, then reach for a weapon. I hit him with a flower vase. Is he alive?"

I pushed the man off me. The back of his head was caved in. There was a pool of blood on the floor.

"No, he's definitely not alive. That's probably a good thing."

Natalie helped me up and led me to the couch. Then she closed the front door that she had left open—no reason the whole town had to know what happened.

"Who was he?" she asked.

"He was from the future and came through the portal. He knew our real names. All he said was that we weren't supposed to be here."

"I heard him say that he was just doing his job," said Natalie.

"Yeah, was him just doing his job supposed to make me feel better about getting killed?"

"So, someone knows we are here," said Natalie.

"And for some reason, they don't want us alive. The question is, will they know that he is dead and we're not? And will they send someone else? I think we have to assume they will."

"How do you think he found us?" asked Natalie. "Do you think they can track people going through the portal?"

"It makes sense. Maybe it's time we act on our desire to leave here," I said.

"But will they be able to track us wherever we go?"

I didn't know how to answer that, so Natalie continued.

"If so," she asked, "will we ever be safe?"

Chapter 24

I searched the man's pockets and found nothing but a little contemporary currency. I hadn't noticed at first that he was wearing a small backpack. Natalie found it near the basement door, and we both looked through it. Other than a few articles of clothing, there was nothing else except a Portal Finder. It looked exactly like the two we already had; one that I recovered from the cave in Hollow Rock and one that we got from the dead Stan Hooper.

"We're collecting Portal Finders," I said.

"Maybe we should have a yard sale," said Natalie.

The fact that we could joke in the presence of a dead man with a bashed-in skull said a lot about where we'd come since all this started.

"What about him?" asked Natalie.

"Let's wrap him in a blanket, and when it gets dark, I'll dig a hole in the backyard. I'd dump him in the shed, but the smell might be overpowering."

Digging a hole to deposit a dead body always looks easy on TV. It's not. To make matters worse, the ground was rocky, so I couldn't dig as deep as I wanted. It took several hours, but I was satisfied with the result. I put some junk from the shed over the spot to keep it from being noticed.

When I finished, I took a shower, sat with Natalie, and

discussed the situation.

"Hopefully, his bosses won't know right away that he failed in his mission, so we might have some time before his replacement shows up," I said.

"Or not," said Natalie. "We're dealing with time travel. They might know already."

"That's true. I hadn't thought of it that way. Even so, the person has to get here. I imagine it will take several days to maneuver the various portals to get to this one."

"That's assuming he arrives *after* the first guy," said Natalie. "What if he arrives before him?"

"You're a ray of sunshine, aren't you?" I remarked.

She laughed.

"But if he did arrive before this guy, wouldn't we be dead already?"

"I think my head hurts," said Natalie.

"Seriously though, we have to be extra-vigilant from now on," I said.

*****

Our vigilance was tested a week later. It was evening, and we were drinking some wine and talking about our respective days when someone knocked on the door. You'd have thought a gun had gone off. I spilled my wine, and we both sat up straight. We looked at each other with a little bit of panic in our eyes.

I reached over and picked up my Glock. These days, I always had it next to me. I motioned for Natalie to go into the kitchen, but she shook her head no. She wasn't going to allow me to face this head-on without her.

I looked at her, and she nodded her head. I opened the door.

I wasn't sure what to make of the group that stood in front of me. There was a woman and a man who looked to be in their thirties. The woman had deep worry lines around her eyes, and the man looked nervous. He was about my height of six feet, with short brown hair. Despite his nervousness, there was a kindness that shone from his eyes. With them was a woman with white hair who had to be in her late seventies or early eighties. It put me slightly at ease until the younger woman asked, "Ray Burton?"

She knew my real name.

I was on edge again. I reached behind my back and pulled out my Glock. I pointed it at her and said, "Who wants to know?"

They all took a step back and put their hands in front of their faces.

"We're friends," said the woman. "The presence of the gun makes me think you've already met one of the assassins sent back to kill you."

"And I repeat. Who are you?"

"My name is Hanna. I'm one of the original six travelers. I was friends with 'Uncle Jim,' Alan, and Herb. I think you knew them."

"And Max," I added.

"Oh, I didn't know that you knew Max, too. Anyway, this is Alex," she said, touching the man gently on the arm. I knew what that touch meant. "And this is Millie. Like you, Natalie, Alex came through the portal by accident. Millie is actually from 1959, but that's a long story. We're here to warn you about the assassins. But I'm guessing that's unnecessary at this point."

I felt a hand on my arm. Natalie was signaling for me to put the gun away. I lowered my arm and put the gun back in my belt.

"I'm sorry for the extreme precautions. Please come in."

We found enough chairs for everyone, and they all accepted glasses of wine. Hanna said the wine was appreciated. It had been a long day.

"You seem to know a lot about us," I said.

"Some, but not a lot," said Hanna. "I have a friend back home who has kept me abreast of events. He's the one who warned me about the assassins."

"She saved me from one in New York," said Alex. "That's how we met."

"What year?" asked Natalie.

"That was 1926. I'm originally from 1973. Since then, it seems like we've been all over."

"Who are the assassins?" I asked.

"They've closed down the Time Travel Project and sent assassins back to 'eliminate'"—she made quotes with her fingers—"everyone who is still traveling. We just heard that they killed two accidental travelers. If you have time, we'll fill you in on the whole story."

"We have all the time in the world," said Natalie, with a chuckle.

With help from Alex, Hanna spent the next couple of hours telling how Alex came through the portal, some of Hanna's experiences, and her friend from home, whose name was Tony. I noticed that Millie didn't say anything. She seemed as mesmerized by the stories as we were.

When they finally explained how they met Millie, Hanna said, "I broke a cardinal rule by telling Millie about time travel, but it was necessary. She's been helpful to us."

Something didn't feel quite right to me about Millie.

Addressing her, I said, "I'm a little amazed that you so readily accepted the explanation of time travel, especially coming from the late fifties. It was a very unimaginative time in American history."

"Just because it's an unimaginative time doesn't mean everyone is unimaginative," she replied.

That made sense.

"Now that you've found us," said Natalie, "what's your plan?"

"We don't really have a plan," replied Hanna. "Whatever we do, we think it would be safer if we stay in a group."

"That makes sense," I said. "But from what you said, it doesn't matter if we stay here or go somewhere else. They know where we are now, but they will also know where we are anytime we access a portal."

"Correct," said Hanna. "So it just means that we have to decide where we all want to go and if that place gives us an advantage against the assassins."

"You are all welcome to stay with us while we decide," said Natalie. "We have a spare bedroom, but someone is going to have to sleep on the couch."

"No need," said Millie. "I saw a quaint little hotel in town. If someone would like to accompany me there, that's where I will spend the night."

Knowing Natalie's popularity in town, she was the logical person to take Millie, but I made sure she took the gun with her.

When Natalie returned, Hanna asked me if I could tell her about the final days of her friends.

"You might say that Herb Wells started it all," I said. "He got drunk one night and told a man named Stan Hooper all about time travel. Stan found out about a portal out west and went through it."

"Herb Wells?" asked Alex. "As in H.G. Wells?"

"That's why he chose that name," said Hanna.

"Cute."

"My involvement was finding a trunk in a cave," I said. "Stan left it. When I found out that Natalie had gone through the same portal accidentally, I went back to find her. The fact that the NSA was on my tail helped me make that decision. Oddly enough, I was asked to find Stan Hooper and kill him since he was going around time and shooting off his mouth. I guess that makes me the first assassin. Natalie and I did find him, and we had to kill

THE YESTERTIME EFFECT

him."

Between Natalie and I, we gave her a fuller picture of the last days of Hanna's fellow travelers.

"The saddest for me was the death of 'Uncle' Jim," I said. "He was a good guy. I never did find out why he was called 'Uncle,'" I added. "They just told me that it was because he was older than the rest of them."

"That's only partly true," said Hanna. "I was the first one to call him that. The reason was he was actually my uncle. He was instrumental in my being accepted into the Time Travel Project. And you are right. He was a good person."

We were all tired, so I showed Alex and Hanna their room. I was impressed by the two of them and mentioned it to Natalie.

"They remind me of us," she said.

"I agree. Did you get Millie settled?"

"I did. She seems like an odd choice for Hanna and Alex to bring with them, but I guess I can understand. She helped them out of a tough situation."

We were all up early the following day and spent the time getting to know each other. Hanna and Alex talked more about their experiences getting here. Natalie went to get Millie from the hotel. After lunch, I asked Hanna a question I had failed to ask the other travelers.

"Could you tell us a little about life where you are from?"

"As I think back on it, it makes me a little sad because I realize how screwed up it is there," said Hanna. "But yes, I will describe it as best I can...."

124

Chapter 25

"It goes against my training to talk about life where I come from," said Hanna. "On the other hand, you've all become fellow travelers. Besides, the chances of us making it home are slim at best. Ray and Natalie, I think you'd be able to relate to my world more than Alex could, and certainly more than Millie. The technology of 2009, when you left, Natalie, and especially 2021, when you left, Ray, was so much more advanced, and the state of the world so different than in 1973, much less Millie's world of 1959. But I won't bother going into the technology because basically everything is different in 2105."

"Flying cars and the like?" asked Natalie.

"That was old news," she answered with a laugh. "Those came into being in the latter half of your century, and with a huge learning curve, I might add. A lot of accidents. But other than some of the flashier inventions, it's not too different from your own time."

"Holographic technology?" I asked.

"Oh, we were far beyond holograms. Artificial Intelligence had reached epic proportions. So much so that much of the technology had to be scaled back. It had become too intelligent. By midway through your century, it was creating far too many problems worldwide. Cloud technology disappeared altogether for a time after a major crash that affected all of society. Banking, power grids, the Internet, and many other vital aspects of civilization collapsed. Individuals, corporations, and governments lost massive amounts of information when the Cloud went down."

"The Cloud?" asked Alex.

"Hard to explain," I said. "It had to do with computers and where the information was stored. Think of it as file cabinets that you couldn't actually touch."

"I'll take your word for it," replied Alex with a laugh.

"I'll go into more detail with you later," said Hanna. "It's complicated. Anyway, everyone just got too dependent on the Cloud. As a result, we went into a worldwide depression that lasted a few years."

"When?" I asked.

"I'm uncomfortable giving you specifics, but it wasn't too many years after you left."

"A lot of people predicted the fall of Cloud technology," I said.

"And did nothing about it," said Hanna. "Well, they were suddenly forced to. They had no choice but to fix it for the sake of the world. That's when the scaling back of technology began to happen. So yes, things are a lot different in my time."

"You still used real money, though," I said.

"Another example of change," said Hanna. "Real money was almost nonexistent by the time of the 'Great Cloud Crash.' That's what they called it. Practically everything was handled electronically. After the Crash, physical money made a comeback and is still used in the 22nd Century. In many ways, the Crash was the best thing to happen to the world. It brought countries together. Oh, there is still the bickering between countries, of course. That will never go away. But there is also the understanding that they have to work together to solve many of the major issues."

"What about the environment?" asked Natalie. "Did we screw that up beyond repair?"

"Ahh," replied Hanna. "Now we get to the nuts and bolts of the Time Travel Project. In short, yes, you screwed it up beyond repair. But a major part of the Project was to change history so that the environment wouldn't get so destroyed."

"Whoa," I said. "I thought the cardinal rule of time travel was not to interfere with the past. After all, isn't that why the assassins are here? Aren't they killing anyone who can be a threat to change time?"

"Yes, that is the basic tenant. Don't interfere with history," said Hanna. "But bear with me. It's kind of involved. Scientists discovered time portals in the 2070s. They first appeared as anomalies in other research they were conducting. That's when the Time Travel Project began. Obviously, at that time, it was just in the research stage, but it was funded by the U.S. government—the NSA, in particular. It's ironic that the NSA of your time was trying to do away with anyone who had knowledge of something that hadn't actually been discovered yet. So when they discovered time portals in the 2070s, was it an accident, or had they been given the idea by the NSA project of the 2021s, which had resulted from the experiments years later?"

"Whoa! That's mind-boggling," said Alex.

"Even to the scientists from my time," replied Hanna. She chuckled. "Most of us tried not to think about it." She turned serious. "Once the scientists determined that time portals were real, that's when the Time Travel Project began to get funding. It was all done secretly. Most people in the government had never heard of it. The environmental crisis had become so dire they began to look at this Project as a way to solve it. It might be enough to turn things around if they could change even just a few things in the late 20th and early 21st Centuries. It all had to be done in such a way that it impacted as few people as possible."

"How is that even possible?" I asked.

"I don't know. That information was a lot higher up the food chain. There were all kinds of rumors going around. One of the more outlandish—but possibly real—had to do with the development of a drug that could be administered to world leaders that would put them under the control of someone we sent back."

"Gee, I can't imagine anything going wrong with that," I said.

"Yeah, me neither. But those were just rumors. There were others mentioned that were equally as unbelievable. But from what my friend Tony sent me, it seems that the powers that be suddenly realized the scariness of all that. It was all too dangerous. That's why they decided to put a stop to the whole Project."

"Were you sent here to start the process of changing the environmental past?" asked Natalie.

"God, no," replied Hanna. "The six of us who were sent back were here simply to collect data on the process of time travel. They were only *talking* about changing the past. They weren't ready to do it. Our job was to find out how stable the portals were, what effect time travel had on our bodies and minds, things like that. It wasn't until after the NSA sent us that they decided to close it down. Frankly, I agree with the decision. There are just too many things that could go wrong. The location of the portals should never be disclosed."

"Do you agree that travelers already here should be eliminated?" I asked.

"In theory," she responded, "they should be stopped in some way, but certainly not eliminated."

"Does that mean they gave up on fixing the environment?" asked Natalie.

"No. Even before the Time Travel Project, scientists were trying to devise ways to artificially turn around environmental destruction. Tony says they've gone back to that."

"Artificially?" asked Alex.

"That's not the right word. They were expanding projects started in your day: creating artificial ocean reefs, demolishing cities and planting forests and creating lakes, things like that. But they are now taking it to a crisis-level emergency. The world won't see the effects for years, but they are working on it."

"Climate change?" asked Natalie.

"Ha, we don't even call it that anymore. The climate already changed. Now we just refer to it as the climate. Nobody has yet figured out how to turn it around. The worst is the water situation. Much of the earth has become barren. By the middle of your century, private companies owned much of the world's water supply. You can imagine the effect that had for most of the world to access water."

"What about space travel?" I asked. "The moon? Mars?"

"We have colonized both. There have been setbacks, but there have also been a lot of great successes. We are colonizing the ocean, as well. We have underwater cities now."

"Do you miss your world?" asked Natalie.

"No. I have no desire to go home. The things I've seen in my travels have been amazing. My world is sterile. This world is alive."

"This is all amazing stuff," said Alex. "I feel as if I was born fifty years too soon."

"What year were you born?" I asked.

"1935."

"You were born thirty-five years before me," I said. "And I don't know if you were born too soon. I think we were all born when we needed to and contributed to the culture of the time. In some ways, the later you were born, the more complicated life became."

"I can attest to that," said Hanna.

I noticed that Millie hadn't said anything. I could only imagine how overwhelming all of this must be to her.

"What's our next step?" asked Alex. "We still have the assassins out there."

"We fight back," replied Hanna.

"How do you propose we do that?" I asked. My time spent in war zones gave me lots of ideas, but I wanted to hear what Hanna was thinking.

"That would probably be more your expertise," said Hanna, which told me that she knew my background. "But my feeling is that we are stronger as a group. A lone assassin against a group of people gives us a definite advantage, don't you think?"

"Not necessarily."

The voice came from the entrance to the kitchen. Standing there was a tall man.

He was pointing a weapon at us.

Chapter 26

"You are not supposed to be here."

"I've heard that before, and I'm already getting tired of it," I said.

"You are especially not supposed to talk about the future," he said.

"I assume you are here to kill us?" I asked.

"I'm sorry, but yes."

He stepped into the room.

Natalie had the fireplace poker in her hand and swung it before the man had a chance to react. The poker hit him hard in the stomach, and he dropped the weapon and doubled over in pain.

I pulled out my Glock and pointed it at him.

"Nice job, Natalie."

"Spur of the moment," she said. "I really didn't think about it."

The man stood up gingerly. He saw me pointing my gun at him.

"Go ahead. Kill me."

"Oh, we will," said Hanna. "And it won't matter. You're an unthinking machine. Your existence means nothing. So your death will mean nothing."

"If that's what you want to believe, then kill me. But you have no idea what you are talking about."

"You kill people," I said. "Isn't that enough of a reason? And you begin your assassination with some robotic bullshit. *'You are not supposed to be here.'* Seriously?"

He went silent, so I continued.

"Hanna is one of your people. She sacrificed everything for your precious Time Travel Project. And this is what she gets? Natalie and Alex came through by accident. Do they deserve to die for that? I'm afraid I have to disagree with Hanna. You are not an unthinking machine. You are a cruel machine."

"So kill me."

I pointed the gun at him.

Why was he so anxious to die? I looked closely at his face. He didn't look much different from Alex or me. He might have been in his early forties, decent shape, and with a somewhat ordinary face. He was clean-shaven.

That was what made me lower the gun. He was clean-shaven. We thought of him as nothing more than a machine. But a machine doesn't care about his appearance. A human does. This man woke up this morning and took the time to shave. Could it be that somewhere inside of him, there was still a touch of humanity?

The others were looking at me. I don't think any of them really wanted me to kill the guy, but I could tell from their expressions that they questioned why I lowered the gun.

"What's your name?" I asked.

He was surprised by the question.

"What?"

"Your name. I'm sure your mother didn't name you 'Unthinking Assassin.'"

"Nathan."

"Okay, Nathan. You said that we have no idea what we are talking about. Enlighten us."

"It doesn't matter now."

"Maybe it does. Try us."

"You see my actions as cruel," began Nathan. "I suppose you can look at it that way, but that's not the purpose of my job. Or at least, that's not how we were trained. I'm realizing now that they weren't honest with us. I thought that what I was doing was the right thing. They told us it was. They explained that there were people who had gone through the portals by mistake and were suffering as a result. They said the kind thing to do would be to put them out of their misery. I've killed two people so far, and in both cases, they were suffering from their accidental pass through the portal. One was in jail with no chance of getting out, and the other was homeless and near death."

He looked at me warily as he talked.

"As for people who went through willingly, including members of the Project," he continued, "we were told that the Time Travel Project was a failure and that you had abused your role. As I look at the five of you, I'm thinking now that maybe you haven't. And it reinforces my feeling that we weren't told the whole story."

"You expect us to believe that?" asked Hanna.

I could understand her anger. She felt betrayed by the very people she had given up her life for.

"I don't expect you to believe anything," answered Nathan. "I'm just answering the question. The fact is, I'm now feeling just as duped as you. When we were sent here, we were told that there were just a few travelers that we had to deal with. All of a sudden, there seem to be a lot more."

"How do you know?" I asked.

"Our Portal Finders show the location of anyone who has gone through a portal, and that number has increased quickly. Also, there are more eliminators...."

"Eliminators?" I interrupted. "Is that what you are called?"

"That's our official title. There were only four of us. I know you killed two of us. Now, there are several more."

"So, more travelers and more assassins ... or eliminators?"

"Yes, and I don't know why. You have to believe me that I'm not a monster. I really thought I was doing the right thing—the merciful thing."

"Why do you all say the line, 'You shouldn't be here' before you kill?" asked Natalie.

Nathan shook his head. "When we were trained, we were told that by saying that line, we would feel somewhat removed from the situation. It would feel like a job and would take all the emotion out of it. It doesn't. In retrospect, it was stupid—just some kind of psychobabble by our instructors. In talking to you, I realize now that I've been given wrong information. I can see that you are all good people. The Project didn't put me here to ease people's suffering. I was sent to kill. It's as simple as that."

Nathan looked as if he meant it.

"Something I don't understand," said Alex.

He didn't seem as angry, and I noticed that the others were beginning to thaw in their opinion of Nathan.

"You were sent here to eliminate the travelers. Assuming you accomplished your mission, the only people left traveling would be the eliminators. How does that change anything?"

"Because I'm going to die, and there is nothing that can stop that."

"Oh my God! You have MMD," said Hanna.

"I do."

"Wow," said Hanna.

"For those of you not familiar with it, which would be all of you except Hanna," said Nathan, "MMD stands for Male Midlife Disease. It was initially diagnosed in the late 21st Century, and no one knows where or how it originated. About three percent of males are born with a gene that kills them when they hit midlife. Anytime between the ages of forty and fifty, the gene can kick in, and you die. Death is instantaneous. You don't feel it coming. One minute you are alive, and the next, you are dead."

"They had to institute laws prohibiting men with MMD from doing certain things once they hit forty," said Hanna. "They can no longer drive, fly, operate equipment, or do anything that could make them a danger to society if they suddenly die. I've never actually met someone with MMD."

"You have now," said Nathan.

"That must be a horrible way to live," I said, "knowing that you could die at any moment. It must really restrict you."

"You get used to it," said Nathan. "You spend your whole life knowing it's going to happen. By the time you hit forty, you are ready for it. Or as ready as you can be. So, all of the eliminators will disappear."

"Another question," said Alex. "You were sent back to kill people who wandered into a portal accidentally, but it's always going to happen. There will always be someone who comes through by mistake, even after you are gone."

"I apologize in advance for the insensitivity, but think of it as cleanup. You clean your house knowing that it will eventually get messy again. All we can do is take care of those who are here now. But that brings up the point I made earlier. Suddenly, there seem to be many more people entering the portals. It's become noisy."

We were out of conversation. What now? What were we going to do about Nathan? Well, someone had to make the decision.

"We are leaving here," I said. "Do you want to come with us?"

I didn't get any outcries from the others, so I was pretty sure I made the right call.

"Thank you," said Nathan. "I didn't expect this. I would be honored to join you. You won't regret it, I promise."

"We better not," said Hanna.

"You should know that I wasn't supposed to kill all of you," he said.

"I don't understand," said Hanna. "I assume not Millie since she hasn't gone through a portal?"

"Not Millie. She's not on my list."

"I think she's not on your list for a different reason," I said.

They all looked at me questioningly, except for Millie, who looked at the floor.

"Do you want to tell them why, Millie?"

Chapter 27

Millie flashed me the hint of a smile.

"I'm impressed," she said. "What gave me away?"

"Several things," I said. "There was something incongruous about an 82-year-old woman who'd spent the last forty years in the same city suddenly hooking up with two people she had just met—two people spinning a wild story of time travel. But I think it really dawned on me when Hanna described life in the 22nd Century. We all had questions for her, except you. On the one hand, it might have simply been a case of you not knowing what to ask. But, on the other hand, silence doesn't seem to be your strong suit. So, I asked myself why you had no questions. It was because you already knew the answers."

"What are you saying?" asked Hanna.

"I'm saying that Millie is one of you. She's a time traveler."

"Whoa," said Alex.

Millie turned to Natalie and said, "Your man is very perceptive."

"I know. That's why I keep him around."

"Does someone want to explain?" asked Alex.

Millie motioned for us all to sit. I had a feeling it was going to be quite a story.

"First of all," she began, "I want to apologize to both of you, Alex and Hanna, for the deception. All of you, really. It's a complicated situation. Bizarre in some ways."

She took a sip of water.

"I come from the year 2136...."

"Thirty-one years after Hanna," said Alex.

"Good math, sonny," said Millie. "I was part of the revival of the Time Travel Project."

"The revival?" asked Hanna.

"Your program was shut down in 2116 or so, but they brought it back twenty years later. My sister and I were part of that."

"Your sister?" asked Alex.

"Yes, Agnes really is my sister. I'll explain in a minute. Anyway, things were getting desperate in the world. We were part of a group twice as large as yours. I was forty-two, and Agnes was forty-eight. Hanna, you were right about the project's original purpose—to go back and make changes. You were also right that they closed it down because they felt it was too dangerous. The thing is, they started it up again. They had to. The world was falling apart, and they had no choice. So we were sent back to make changes. We were told that the initial Project was a massive failure but that they had improved on it."

"Wait a minute," said Alex. "That means you must have known about the assassins. But you stayed silent."

"I didn't know about the assassins," said Millie. "We were never told."

"How did you end up in Atlanta for forty years?" asked Natalie.

"An accident. Simply stated, we lost our Portal Finder. We were out searching for a local portal in a long-abandoned mine. I was holding it when I tripped, and it fell down a shaft. We tried everything to get it back but were told that the shaft was hundreds of feet deep. So the Portal Finder was gone forever. That was forty years ago."

"You must have been devastated," said Natalie.

"That doesn't even come close to how we felt. We had only been in Atlanta for a couple of weeks, and it was just our first stop. So, we hadn't even accomplished anything yet. Then, with the Portal Finder gone, we lost all contact with our team."

"There were two of you," I said. "Didn't you have two Portal Finders?"

Millie made a face.

"It was our fault. We insisted on traveling as a pair, so they felt that we only needed one. Portal Finders are expensive, and the project was already over budget, so they found a way to save some money. The cheap bastards."

"Wouldn't they send anyone after you?" I asked.

"Because we weren't accessing portals, they would have assumed we were dead. So there was no reason to check on us. We were stuck in time."

I noticed that Alex and Hanna weren't saying anything, but their expressions spoke volumes. They were pissed. Millie had deceived them. I wasn't sure that she would ever regain their trust.

"It hit both of us hard," continued Millie. "I was able to move on with my life, but Agnes wasn't. She got a job as a librarian and found a place to live, eventually buying the house you saw. But that was the extent of her existence from that point on. She lost all interest in life. Then, a few years ago, I began to notice that she was slipping. Her mind lost its sharpness soon after she retired. In recent months, the dementia became worse."

"And you just left her and took off on your own?" asked Hanna with a sharpness in her voice.

"She understood," answered Millie.

"I doubt that," said Hanna.

"Anyway," said Millie, turning away from Hanna, "I got a job with the Atlanta police department, and that's where I stayed for the next forty years."

"I don't get it," I said. "If you were a time traveler, weren't you some sort of scientist? Couldn't you have put your knowledge to better use over those forty years? Couldn't you have tried to fulfill at least a part of your mission?"

"I wasn't a scientist. I was an activist. It was felt that I would have a better chance of making change happen than a scientist would."

"Then why didn't you?" asked Natalie. I noticed that her voice had an edge to it now. Millie wasn't making any friends.

"Simply put, I lost interest. I didn't feel that there was anything I could do. So, I fell into life in Atlanta in the 20th Century. I felt guilty abandoning my mission, but I also didn't feel as if there was anything I could do."

"How did you find us?" asked Alex.

"Again, I apologize...."

"Stop apologizing!" said Hanna in a voice louder than necessary.

Millie put her head down. When she lifted it, I detected a tear in her eye. Real or fake? I didn't know anymore.

"I found you both by accident. Before we left, we were all shown pictures of the original six travelers. We were told that four of you were dead but that you weren't. After forty years, I might not have remembered the picture of you, Hanna. But when I saw you both in the bus station, I knew you didn't fit in with the rest of the people. Then I realized that you seemed familiar to me. My mind has always been sharp. I simply made the connection. I was pretty sure I was right. A word of advice: You need to work on integrating with the people of the time, Hanna. You seemed awkward."

"Don't you dare try to give me time travel advice!" snapped Hanna. "I've been doing this for twelve long years. You sat on your ass and gave up! You have no right...."

She stood up and strode from the room. After glaring at Millie, Alex followed Hanna.

Millie looked from Natalie to me, then said, "I handled that poorly."

"You deceived them, then insulted them," said Natalie. "Yes, you handled that poorly."

"I'm going to go back to my hotel," said Millie. "I'm drained. I'll get my coat."

She walked into the kitchen and retrieved her coat, and without another word, she walked out of the house.

"Should I follow her to make sure she gets there safely?" I asked.

Natalie shook her head. "I think we should just let her go. We'll see what tomorrow brings."

Hanna and Alex entered the room. Hanna had been crying.

"I'm sorry," she said. "That was all too much for me to take."

"No reason to apologize," said Natalie. "I probably would have done the same thing."

"I don't think I can be around her anymore," said Hanna.

"I think she knows that," I said. "If I had to guess, I'll bet she tells us to continue without her, and she ends up going back to Atlanta."

I was close. Natalie went to check on Millie the next morning and came back to say that she was gone.

"Her room was empty," said Natalie. "She left without paying her bill. I took care of it, but Millie is gone."

"It's not just Millie that is gone," said Hanna entering the room. "My Portal Finder is missing. I've looked everywhere. It was in the kitchen."

"Millie went into the kitchen for her coat before she left," I said.

Hanna shook her head in resignation.

"Millie stole it."

Chapter 28

Millie was excited. After forty years, she finally had a Portal Finder. She could escape this ignorant time and go somewhere more appealing. But where? It had to be sometime in the future. Of all the times to get stuck in, she had to end up in the 1900s. Besides the ignorance, it was a boring time. Were people not interested in anything more than the most mundane activities? She had to get somewhere more technologically advanced. The early 2000s were the beginning of the interesting time for her. She could live with that. It was technologically advanced but not yet overcome by its technology.

She was on the early train to London. She was sorry that she skipped out without paying her bill, but she wanted her departure to be as unnoticed as possible. The hotel people would get over it. It wasn't like she had stolen anything.

And then there were Hanna and Alex. She truly felt sad to leave them. She had enjoyed their company. Especially Alex. He was a good person and interesting to talk to. Hanna was different. She liked her, but Hanna was jaded from twelve years of traveling. It wouldn't have taken her much longer before recognizing Millie for who she was.

Hanna was right. It wasn't right for her to try to give Hanna advice. It might have been true that Hanna seemed out of place, but it was egotistical of Millie to assume that she knew better than

Hanna. The only reason Millie could pull it off was because she'd been in the same place for forty years. She hadn't been traveling. Well, she'd make up for it now. She'd see how much she could cram in before she died.

Alex was cute, but it was Ray who fascinated her. The man had an impressive background. If she were thirty years younger, she'd be making a play for him. She couldn't care less about the actress. Yes, Millie knew her story. Frankly, the woman was lucky that Ray had been starstruck enough to try and help her. Without Ray, the woman would've been eaten alive in 1870.

It didn't matter now. The fact was, everything about her was a lie, and they would have eventually discovered it. What would they have done? They had an eliminator with them now. Once he knew the truth, he would have felt that it was his responsibility to kill her.

She thought back to that day so long ago. Was it really forty years? It was Agnes's idea. Millie was excited at the thought of it but didn't think they could really go through with it. But Agnes insisted that they could get away with stealing the Portal Finder.

It belonged to their friend Jane, an anthropologist chosen for the Project. Against the rules, Jane had told Millie and Agnes all about her time travel training and had shown them the workings of the Portal Finder. It was all Jane's fault. If she hadn't been so free with the information, Agnes never would have latched onto the idea of stealing the device. It didn't take long for Agnes to convince Millie. Think of the adventures they could have!

A few nights before Jane was supposed to leave, Millie and Agnes took her out for a farewell drink. One drink turned to many for Jane while Millie and Agnes watched their intake carefully. Finally, they helped a very drunk Jane home and put her to bed. Then they stole the Portal Finder and some files of information. That's where she saw the pictures of the first travelers, including Hanna. The following day, they were on their way to Atlanta, to a portal Jane had planned to access.

Millie and Agnes entered the portal together, hand-in-hand, knowing that they needed to be connected to land together. The world they entered was wondrous. Everything was so green and vibrant. All thoughts of the deception they used to get there disappeared. Jane soon became nothing but a memory.

Their new life was wonderful for the first week, but they soon tired of Atlanta post World War I. They needed more excitement, so they consulted the Portal Finder. Much to their surprise, there was another portal not far away located in an old mine that would take them back to the 1800s. The idea of America in the 1800s excited them, so they found the abandoned mine and broke in. But on their way to the portal, tragedy struck when they dropped the Portal Finder into the deep mineshaft.

The devastation they felt was overwhelming. They were stuck in Atlanta in 1919.

The more practical of the two, Millie pushed on, getting the job with the Atlanta police department. Agnes tried to move on, becoming a librarian, but the spark had been extinguished.

Millie occasionally wondered what had happened to Jane. Had she been given another Portal Finder and been allowed to keep her position with the Project? Probably not. They probably dismissed her for telling Millie and Agnes about it. Their actions had destroyed Jane's dream. Millie should have felt guilty, but she didn't. Shit happens. But shit had also happened for Millie and Agnes. Maybe it was karma.

Not being part of the Project, Millie hadn't heard about the eliminators sent out after the first group. Now, if Millie entered a portal, would they be after her? It was a good possibility.

If so, she would have to plan her next move very carefully.

Chapter 29

It was time to decide our future, but it would have to wait a few hours. The disappearance of Millie was the predominant topic of discussion during the day. At our invitation, Nathan joined us that morning. He had gone back to his hotel room the night before a troubled man. The realization that he hadn't been told the truth about his job had been gnawing at him for some time. Meeting us just confirmed his suspicions. We all felt comfortable including him in our group.

Hanna and Alex were both upset about being duped by the old lady. I tried to offer some perspective, but it didn't go well.

"All I'm saying," I explained, "is that she might not have been out to use you. From my limited observation, I think she genuinely liked you both. Holding back the information about herself was a major error and one she probably regretted."

"I disagree," said Hanna. "What would have been her reason for withholding the information that she was a traveler? Okay, in the beginning, maybe, but why not tell us once she got to know us? What was she hiding?"

We looked at Nathan.

"I can't help you," he said. "I was sent a few years after the first group of travelers—your group, Hanna. Millie said she was part of the second group of travelers. I don't know anything about them."

Natalie hadn't said much to that point, so I asked her if she had any thoughts.

"I do," she said. "It's one that just came to me a minute ago. She told us that she wasn't a scientist."

"Right," I said. "She said she was an activist."

"Hanna," said Natalie, "I know that your group's purpose was to log the effects of time travel, but were you all scientists?"

"Scientists and doctors, for the most part. But I wasn't either one. I was a grad student studying for a doctorate in behavioral psychology."

"That counts," said Natalie. "Here's what I'm getting at. Time travel is a science. The powers that be would only want the smartest people in specific disciplines to be involved in it. Scientists and doctors. They'd want people who wouldn't put their emotions first. Emotions could lead to people finding out that you are a time traveler. This second group was meant to influence the world in a positive way—to get leaders to make different decisions for the environment, right?"

"Yes," said Hanna.

"That's a tricky proposition," Natalie continued. "Who would you *not* want to be involved?"

"Someone with an emotional stance," I said. I had a feeling I knew where this was going.

"Activism certainly has its place in the world, but who would send an activist back in time?" asked Natalie. "Everything about activism smacks of emotion. It's the last person you would want to send in this case."

"So, she's a fraud?" asked Alex.

"I think you hit on it, Natalie," said Hanna. "I don't think she's supposed to be here. You're right; an activist is the last person they would send. But she couldn't pretend to be a scientist because someone might have asked her something she couldn't answer."

"If that's the case," said Nathan, "she will become a target of the eliminators the moment she accesses a portal."

We picked up a load of fish and chips for dinner and brought it back. Then, we all sat in the living room and ate while we discussed our next move.

"Before you all showed up," I said, "Natalie and I had decided that it was time to leave here. It was a fun diversion, but it's not who we are. Maybe we'll never find our way home or find the perfect place, but it's worth trying. What do you three think?"

"I'll follow the group," said Nathan. "I appreciate you including me, so I'll go anywhere you want. Besides, my opinion isn't worth a lot. I have MMD. I could be dead next week."

"Well, that was sobering," I said.

"Sorry."

"Nothing to be sorry about. I'm not sure what I would do in your shoes."

"It's not that bad. I've known it my whole life, so I'm ready."

We took a moment to digest that, then Hanna said, "Once I heard about the assassins, all I could think about was to help Alex and warn you and Natalie."

"And we thank you," I said.

"I hadn't yet thought about what to do after. Alex?"

"Me neither," he said. "But I do think we should stick together. I like all of you. I think with Millie gone, it opens up our options."

"I agree," I said. "Here's my thought. We all grew up in the United States. Granted, at different times, but I think we would all feel more comfortable in a familiar environment. So, my thought is that we travel to the States. I realize that Hanna and Alex just came from there, though."

"I like that idea," said Alex. "If we do that, I suggest going over there now and finding a portal from there, considering we already have current passports."

"Natalie and I don't," I said. "We came here from the 1940s."

"I can check the Portal Finder later and see what's there," said Hanna, "but it might be easier to see what portals are available worldwide. From that list, we can decide what era we want to access, go there, and then go to the States. Then, we might not have to worry about passports."

"That makes sense," I said. "Here's the question. If we have a choice of eras, what would be the best one? We have all kinds of things to consider, and I honestly don't know the best choice. Natalie and I were hoping to arrive soon after I left, sometime in the 2020s. However, the NSA was gunning for me, so we would have to give that serious consideration. Alex, you came from 1973. No offense, but I lived through the '70s, '80s, and '90s and have no desire to do it again."

"Amen," said Natalie.

"Hanna, you and Nathan come from the 22nd Century, and Hanna, you've made it clear that you don't want to go back."

"And I don't either," said Nathan. "However, as I said before, I will go anywhere you all decide."

"Where does that leave us?" asked Alex.

"Beats the hell out of me," I said.

Chapter 30

Natalie and I continued the discussion in bed that night, but the more we talked, the more confusing it became. We agreed that we wanted to go back to the States, but when?

We had already been in the West in the 1800s. That was out.

If we went back to the 21th Century, it would have to be after I left. Then we had the issue of the NSA looking for me. Also, we now knew about the Great Cloud Collapse. Hanna wouldn't give us the date, but it didn't matter. We knew it would happen, and Hanna knew the exact date it would happen. So what would we do with the information?

The other problem with that time was the recognition factor. Natalie O'Brien was a major star. So if she were recognized, we'd have to come up with a story, and time travel couldn't be a part of it.

Something we hadn't talked about as a group but was a concern to me was landing at a time when any of us were still alive. I just felt that it could create problems in the long run. Alex was born in 1935 and disappeared in 1973. Any time after 1973 would work—for him. But what about Natalie and me? I was born in 1970 and didn't disappear until 2021. Natalie was born in 1979 and disappeared in 2009. The fact that I was twenty years older in actual age was one of those weird aspects of time travel—when she went through the portal as opposed to when I went through. It also couldn't be too close to 1935 because we wouldn't want Alex to be alive when he is born.

The implications were staggering, and it had us going in circles. We finally decided that arriving sometime after 2021 would be best for all concerned despite the Cloud issue and the NSA. It wouldn't overlap any of us, age-wise, including Hanna, who wouldn't be born until 2082.

Of course, that all depended on us finding a portal to take us there, and the chances of that were slim at best.

We ended up sleeping only a couple of hours, and when we arrived in the kitchen the next morning, the others commented on our appearance. We explained our conversation. Hanna and Alex said they had a similar discussion but managed a few more hours of sleep.

"I slept like a baby for the first time in months," said Nathan, getting a laugh from the rest of us.

There was something about Nathan that I liked. Getting beyond the fact that he almost killed us, there was a humanity to him that was beginning to shine through. He had a sense of humor, and he was intelligent. I truly believed that he thought he was doing the right thing in becoming an eliminator.

"I think your conclusions make sense," said Hanna. "That would probably be the ideal solution. But, unfortunately, getting there will be the issue. I was looking at the portal map that my friend Tony sent me. It's not going to help us much. So, this morning I turned on one of the Portal Finders to get a sense of what was available to us. There's not a lot. The closest ones take us further back in time than we want. I'm talking about the 1700s. A couple could be promising, but one is in the middle of Vietnam. Vietnam in 1959 is not a good place to visit. Another is smack in the Amazon rainforest in Brazil."

"Difficult to get to," I said.

"The portal in Hollow Rock, Arizona is open," said Hanna,

"but that would be a bad idea. The two of you already accessed it, so to go through it again could be bad. If you arrived after you had already left, at worst, it could be confusing. But what if you arrived while you were still there? Catastrophic, I would think. I'm not even sure the laws of physics would allow it, but we don't want to take the chance."

"I had enough of that place, anyway," said Natalie.

"I'm sure," said Hanna, "So, the best option seems to be Australia. There's a portal there that will take us back to 1901. That's not too bad. The portal is not anywhere close to a city, so we may have to do some driving to find it. According to Tony's map, there seem to be a lot of options from there, but it's not clear where the options take us."

"You could always just stay right here," said Nathan.

"That might work for a while," I said, "but I'd hate to end up like Millie and be stuck here for the next twenty years."

"We're all travelers," said Hanna. "Granted, most of you weren't willing travelers, but the fact is, that's what we are now. We all have a taste of traveling in our blood. I don't know about you, but I can't sit around."

We all nodded in agreement.

"Then I say we get going," I said. "I'll leave a note for Hal, but now that we know about the eliminators, I'll have to hide it and hope he finds it."

"Can we leave him a Portal Finder, too?" asked Natalie. "We have enough of them that we can spare one. That way, he might be able to find the portal, in case we want to leave him a message. Or...."

"Or he might come through the portal," said Nathan. "I heard that the NSA back then eliminated a lot of people who they thought were connected to time travel in any way. So, he might be on the run like you were, Ray. I read up on it a bit. It's amazing how paranoid the NSA was back when they began to get a whiff of time travel. They spent a lot of money investigating it. And then how quickly they closed down the section, eliminating anyone who might be able to connect them to it. They didn't want their money expenditure to be revealed."

"Yes, that's what I experienced," I said.

"Okay, then," Natalie said. "We're agreed? We're going to Australia?"

We were on our way to London the next day.

PART THREE

Chapter 31

SAXMUNDHAM, ENGLAND—2023

Hal March felt light-headed and sat down on the floor of the basement. Ray *had* left him a message. How stupid that he didn't think of looking for it before.

Besides the excitement of finding a note, Hal was still reeling a bit from killing the two NSA agents. Since no police had knocked on his door, he felt safe that the killings had gone undetected. But he knew he couldn't stay in the house long. Maybe Ray's note would help him devise his next plan.

The note was typed but with Ray's signature at the bottom. Finally, Hal was feeling a little better. He stood up and went upstairs with the message. He got a beer from the fridge and sat on the couch. He wanted to be comfortable for this. The house still reeked of bleach, bringing back the memories of his earlier encounter. But he no longer cared. He had been stressed for too long, and it was time to think only about himself. He took a sip of beer and began reading.

Dear Hal,

I hope you find this. I couldn't leave it out in the open, and I tried to think of where you might find it. The copy of Antiques, Etc. *seemed the only logical solution.*

Hal thought to himself that if he'd been more aware, he would have found this note six months ago when Ray left his final package of material. Would it have made a difference, time-wise? Probably not.

We have three guests staying with us. Two of them are Hanna and Alex. Hanna is one of the original six travelers. They came to warn us about something we should all be concerned about. It seems that similar to the NSA of the 21st century closing down shop, the NSA of the 22nd century decided (will decide? Past tense or future tense?) to close down the Project. They have sent assassins from that century to "eliminate" anyone who has gone through a portal. They want all traces of the time travel experiment gone. We've already killed one of the assassins, as did Hanna and Alex, but there will be more. So, for us, it's time to move on. Our third guest is an assassin who had a change of heart.

I'm telling you this for three reasons. First, this will be my final communication from here. We are deciding where to go after this. Second, your life is in danger. I'm told that the NSA from 2023 expanded their search and decided to eliminate anyone who knew about the portals. That would include you. If that's the case, you need to go into hiding.

And that brings up the third reason. We have the extra Portal Finder that we stole from Stan Hooper when we killed him. I'm leaving it for you. If things get difficult and you have to escape that century, you are welcome to join us. I will program our next location into the Portal Finder. If you decide to stay in your century, the programmed location will tell you where we are, and I will try to find a place to leave a message for you.

You can find the Portal Finder under a floorboard in the bedroom closet. Included are instructions on how to use it. It's pretty simple.

If this is the last time we are in touch with each other, it's been an honor knowing you. Otherwise, maybe we'll meet again, or at least be in touch with each other again.

Take care and STAY SAFE!
Ray

Hal put down the note and his beer and hurried into the bedroom. He opened the closet and quickly found the floorboard in question. He pried up the board using his Swiss Army Knife and found the Portal Finder.

Hal had heard about it from Ray but had never seen one. This one was wrapped in plastic, along with the operating instructions. He unwrapped it and hesitated. He was nervous. Turning it on was suddenly a significant event. Would it still work after all these years? He took a deep breath and, following the instructions, turned it on. He wasn't sure what he was expecting, but it was somewhat anticlimactic. It didn't make a noise, but lights of all kinds began to blink. On the front was a small display screen. He followed the instructions to show the address that had been programmed. It was in Australia. A note also told him it had to be accessed from Ray's time, not 2023.

Hal sat on the floor. He had some decisions to make. What were his options? He couldn't stay where he was. Others would follow the two agents that he killed. He couldn't go home. There was only one choice, and he knew it. He had known it from the moment he had to leave Boston.

He had to go through the portal.

Chapter 32

Three days had passed since Hal's reading of the note. It was three days of speculation and self-evaluation. But, mostly, it was three days of fear. Were more NSA guys coming after him? Would the two in the shed be discovered? He had covered them in lime and didn't know if that would camouflage the smell, but he had to try something. So far, there hadn't been much of a scent, thanks in part to the constant cold rain that never seemed to let up. The rain also kept folks inside, which would make it harder for them to smell it.

His speculation centered on where Ray and Natalie were now, and his self-evaluation was whether he dared to go through a portal. The fact that he could only access the Australian portal from 1959 or 1960 was probably good. He'd never make it to Australia now. The NSA would have his face on every computer at every entrance or exit port.

Just in case he had to move quickly, he kept his small backpack in the basement near the portal entrance. Then, if he had to use the portal because he was running for his life, he could just pick up the bag and walk through.

But that was the question. Could he just walk through? He

got the hint of an answer a couple of days after killing the NSA agents. He was in the pub talking to Wilfred and the others. Hal had become accepted by the small group of old-timers by virtue of the fact that he often paid for the beers.

"I have to ask you, Yank," Wilfred said. "Have we met before?"

"Well, yes. I've been coming in here every day."

"No, I don't mean, have we ever met? I'm not daft. I mean, did we meet sometime in the distant past? Ever since you started showing up here, I've had the feeling that we met a long time ago."

"Just like he thinks he met that movie star, Natalie O'Brien," said one of the others with a guffaw.

Hal knew precisely what it meant. The only way Wilfred would think that he met Hal was if Hal ended up going back in time. Which means he went back. *Went or will go?* Where did free will come in? Did this mean that Hal had no choice but to go back in time? But what if he decided not to? Would Wilfred's memory change?

Whoa! That was way too much to think about.

"I'm afraid it must have been someone who looked like me, the poor guy."

That got some laughs from the others.

He stayed for a while, drinking with Wilfred and his friends. But he knew his real motivation. He didn't want to go home. Home reminded him that there were two bodies in the shed. It also reminded him that the NSA was probably still after him. But, most of all, the portal was there, and he had to decide whether he was going through it.

Hal finally convinced himself to go home when the others became so drunk, their accents became exaggerated, and he could no longer understand them. He left the building into the night air and realized that he was also a bit drunk. There was still a cold drizzle coming down. He took off his hat and let the rain soak his head and roll down his neck. Maybe it would sober him up. He thought about picking up some fish and chips, but his stomach was reeling from the beer. It would be best to hold off.

He stopped across the street from his house. Again, the lights were off, but he didn't see any flashlight beams this time. He looked around. All seemed quiet. Except....

A car was parked on the side of the road about a block away. It's not like cars didn't park on the road, but there was something about that one. He couldn't put his finger on it, but something wasn't right. He saw the bright end of a cigarette. Someone was in the car.

His decision about the portal may have been made for him. He quickly crossed the road and entered his house through the back door. No one was inside. He left the lights off. He ran into the bedroom, stripped off his clothes, and replaced them with dry ones. He would have loved to have taken a shower, but he knew he didn't have time for it.

Everything he needed was in the backpack in the basement. He turned on the living room light. He may as well let them know he's home. That way, he would know for sure if he was being stalked.

Hal opened the basement door and turned on the light. He shut the door behind him and sat on the top step. Was it just his imagination about the car? Was he taking all these precautions for nothing?

Then he heard it. The back door opened. Hal crept down the stairs to the basement.

And then all hell broke loose!

From under the door at the top of the stairs, Hal saw the flashing lights of police cars. They must have pulled up right outside his kitchen window. Then, he heard the front door burst open and his name being called. A dozen or more people were suddenly running through his house, and the basement door was jerked open.

He had no choice now. He picked up the backpack and pushed past the barrier he'd set up.

He ran toward the wall. The noise of the pursuers was all around him.

Suddenly it was quiet and dark.

The noise was gone. The people were gone, and it was dead quiet.

He had done it. Hal had gone through a time portal!

It was pitch black in the basement. He took out his mini flashlight and looked for a light switch. There was a lamp in front of him, and he turned it on.

The basement didn't look too different. It was unfinished. But of course, he knew that. He was the one who finished it. The pile of material Hal had left for Ray over the past six months was sitting there, but it looked as if it had been gone through. Strange.

The basement smelled musty. But then, basements always smelled musty. It was time to check out the upstairs.

He pulled out his gun as he climbed the stairs. He was pretty sure no one would be there, but it was best to play it safe.

He reached the top of the stairs and pushed open the door. The house was dark.

Hal started to walk across the kitchen to turn on a light when he was hit with something hard from behind!

He fell to the floor, then rolled as the heavy item slammed the floor next to him. He rose to his knees, only to be jumped on from behind. The person was screeching like an animal. It was a woman!

Hal flipped her over his head, and she hit the floor with a thud. But she was up in a second and attacking him from the front.

"Wait...." He tried to say, but a hand grabbed his ear and

pulled him to the ground. The woman jumped on his chest and began pounding on him. He pushed her off, and she slid across the floor and hit the stove.

"Stop!" he yelled. But it did no good. The woman was like a crazed animal. She jumped at him again. This time he was ready. He punched her in the face with all the strength he had left.

She dropped to the floor unconscious.

Chapter 33

Hal sat on the floor for a minute, trying to catch his breath. What had just happened? One minute the police and the NSA were closing in, and the next, he was being attacked by a madwoman.

Every muscle in his body ached. He looked around for what hit him. It was a heavy lamp. The woman was strong. He was going to have a massive bruise on his back. He checked himself for other injuries. Except for a few scratch marks and facial bruises, he was okay.

He stood up slowly and looked at the woman. He regretted punching her, but it was the only way to stop her. She had a bruise where he hit her, and her nose was bleeding. He was pretty sure she'd have a black eye by tomorrow.

What to do with her? He should try to stop the nosebleed, but not until she was tied up. There was no way he was going to deal with that again. He looked through kitchen drawers until he found some rope. As he tied her to a radiator in the living room, he studied her closely.

She looked to be in her forties, but it was a hard forties. She hadn't aged gracefully. Her hair, shoulder-length light brown mingled with gray, was a mess and totally out of control. It looked as if she had stuck her finger in a light socket. She was average height but thin—almost starving thin. Despite that, Hal knew from recent experience that she was strong.

He found a rag and soaked it in warm water. Her nose had stopped bleeding, but her face was covered in blood. He used the rag to wipe off the dried blood. As he did, he looked at her closer. Her skin was soft. Yes, she was hard looking, but she hadn't always been. Hal imagined that she had once been quite attractive.

What was her story?

Well, he wouldn't find out immediately. She was down for the count. Good. That would give him time to figure out things, such as: When did he arrive?

Hal turned on a couple of lights. If anyone asked, he would explain that he was a friend of Ray's. He had to remember that Ray and Natalie were now going by the last name of Bean.

He looked around the kitchen. It looked like the kitchen he knew, except that the appliances were older. On the wall was a calendar given out by a local business. September 1959 was displayed. Good. At least he now had a reference point. The question was, what was the date now?

The Portal Finder! That would tell him the date. He turned it on.

I'm becoming an old pro with this, he thought.

May 1960. If the calendar on the wall reflected when they left, they had been gone about eight months. He could find out for sure at the pub. He remembered that Natalie had worked there. Would he see a young Wilfred?

He heard the woman stir and then heard her swear.

"Fuck," she said quietly.

Hal went into the living room. She looked up at him with undisguised hatred.

"You're awake," Hal said.

She was silent.

"I'm sorry I had to hit you. It's nothing personal. I just don't like being attacked."

"You're American," she said. There was a hint of surprise in her voice.

"I am. I'm from Boston. Not originally, but for the last thirty years or so."

The last thirty years? That wasn't exactly right if this was 1960.

"My name is Hal March. Are you a traveler?"

Getting no response, he asked, "Are you an assassin?"

"Do I look like an assassin?"

"I don't know. What do assassins look like?"

"Fuck you."

"We seem to have gotten off on the wrong foot. Of course, the fact that you attacked me might have something to do with that. But putting that aside for the moment, what are you doing here? Particularly, what are you doing here in this house? One might think that you are just squatting in an empty house, but since you also have an American accent, I don't see you as a homeless Brit. So that tells me that it's something more."

She had gone silent again.

"Whoever you think I am, I'm not. But I think I know who—or what—you are because the chances of you being in this particular house and not being a time traveler are minuscule. Are you a time traveler?"

She wasn't talking.

"Okay, the fact that you didn't deny it tells me that you are. So, let's try a name association game. I will list a few names, and you tell me if they are familiar. Ray Burton."

Nothing.

"Natalie O'Brien."

Nothing.

"Jim Lawrence. Also known as Uncle Jim."

A slight head movement. Hal knew he was on the right track.

"Herb Wells."

More signals of recognition.

"I worked with Uncle Jim," said Hal. "Specifically, he worked for me. You couldn't find a more likable guy. I knew Herb Wells, but I wouldn't put him in the same category as Uncle Jim."

He had an idea based on Ray's note.

"How about Hanna?"

That did it.

"Is Hanna alive?" she asked.

"I haven't met her, but according to a note I received, she's alive and was staying here for a short time. Unfortunately, we've missed them."

And then it dawned on him.

"I was told that there were originally six travelers from your Project. I know that four of them are dead. In his note, Ray told me that Hanna was the fifth. No one knew what happened to the sixth, but I knew it was a woman. I never learned her name. Are you the missing sixth time traveler?"

Hal saw her shoulders sink.

"My name is Simone."

"If I untie you, Simone, do you promise not to attack me?"

She nodded.

"I'll take you at your word."

He untied the knot and freed Simone's arms. She rubbed them and then felt her face.

"I'm afraid your face won't look very good tomorrow. Again, I apologize, but I had little choice."

"I understand. So, who are you, and how do you know about the Time Travel Project?"

"It's kind of a long story."

"I have time."

"Ha. A good one. Anyway, a couple of years ago, I wouldn't have believed any of this. And then I met Ray Burton."

Hal explained about Ray discovering the chest in a cave and investigating it, and how it led to Ray meeting Hal and some of the time travelers. He then told her about Ray going back in time to rescue Natalie.

"That was stupid," said Simone.

"It was stupid, but it has worked out. The last I knew, Ray and Natalie were staying here, and we would pass information back and forth through the portal. That communication suddenly ended six months ago. In the meantime, the NSA of my time decided to eliminate anyone who had come in contact with time travel information. At the same time, so to speak, I finally got word from Ray that they had to escape some assassins sent back in time and that a couple named Hanna and Alex were with them. He made a point of telling me that Hanna was one of the original six. The assassins after them are different from the assassins who were after me. Supposedly, his assassins are targeting all of you who were part of the Project and anyone who might have entered a portal accidentally."

Simone's attention was drifting, so Hal asked her if she was hungry.

"I am."

"Tell you what. I saw some cash in one of the drawers when I was looking for rope to tie you up with. I know where there is a good pub. It's here now and will still be there in 2023. Let's go over and eat something. You can tell me your story there, or we can eat, and you can tell me when we come back. Either way, you need food."

Simone didn't protest but wanted to take a few minutes to freshen up. Meanwhile, Hal emptied the drawer of money—making sure it was current money.

When she came out of the bathroom, her hair was brushed, and her face was washed. She looked like a new person—a new person with the beginnings of a fist-sized bruise on her face.

As they left the house, Hal said, "I'll be interested in hearing your story."

"You might regret it," answered Simone.

"Why?"

"It's about as horrible as you can imagine."

Chapter 34

When they entered the pub, Hal picked out Wilfred immediately. He almost felt dizzy looking at him.

"What's wrong?" asked Simone

"See that young guy playing darts? His name is Wilfred. Just a few hours earlier, I was talking to an 85-year-old Wilfred. Now I'm watching him at twenty-five. It's a little overwhelming."

"I can imagine. I haven't experienced that yet. Not sure I want to. I'm not sure I want to experience any of it anymore."

"Tired of time travel?"

"Tired of life."

A waitress came over and took their order. As she was leaving, the young Wilfred sauntered over.

"Haven't seen you in here before. Passing through? Fancy a game of darts?"

"No, thank you. We need to eat something. But maybe you can help me. Your name wouldn't be Wilfred, would it?"

"How did you know?"

"I'm friends with Ray and Natalie Bean. They told me to stop by if I was in the area. They even gave me a key. So we came by, but they seem to be gone. Did they move away?"

"Aye, about eight months ago. They said they were going to Australia. Now, how did you know my name?"

"I know that Natalie worked here. She talked about a young

bloke named Wilfred. She said she fancied him. Don't get me wrong. She loves Ray and would never think of playing around. But she said this Wilfred bloke was really cute. But don't tell her I said that."

"No chance of that. I think they are gone for good."

"I guess we'll just stay for a couple of days, then head home."

"You do that."

Hal wasn't sure if Wilfred even heard them. He walked away on Cloud 9.

"You made his day," said Simone.

"He told me sixty years from now that Natalie fancied him. How did he get that idea? Who's to say it wasn't me who planted it in his head? So for the next sixty years, he can dream about Natalie."

"That was a kind thing to do."

Hal noticed Simone's hands shaking.

"Are you okay?"

"No. I'll never be okay."

"Want to tell me?"

"When we get back to the house. For now, I just want to soak this in. A sense of normalcy. It's been years since I experienced that."

Hal decided to let the comment go. They spent the next hour eating, drinking beer, and people-watching. But toward the end of the hour, Simone began shaking again, and she asked to leave.

Walking back to the house, she suddenly had an episode where she couldn't breathe. Hal had her sit on a bench with her head between her knees. After a few minutes, she was ready to continue, but Hal noticed that the shaking hadn't stopped. What could have affected her that much?

Once inside the house, Hal lit a fire and gave Simone a blanket to cover herself on the couch. Hal sat in a chair opposite.

"If you're not ready to talk about it, that's okay," he said.

"No. I need to talk about it. Back where I come from, the doctors would call it therapy."

"Where I come from too," said Hal.

"You said you are from 2023?" asked Simone.

"I am."

"I'm from 2105. In some ways, our worlds probably weren't that different."

"Very different from this life," said Hal.

He saw her eyes grow distant, and he knew she was about to start her story.

"The first four years of time travel were fun," she began. "There were a few tense situations, but nothing I hadn't been trained for."

She took a deep breath.

"But I've spent the last eight years in hell."

Chapter 35

PARIS, FRANCE—1813

This was going to be tricky. No, it was worse than that. It was a terrible idea. When they handed out assignments, early 19th Century France was added to Simone's list for the simple reason that she had listed "French" under languages spoken. It wasn't exactly a lie. She had taken French in high school and college, but her skills were rudimentary, at best.

She had desperately wanted to be part of the Time Travel Project and had looked for any advantage to getting on the list. But when all was said and done, her French-language "skills" had nothing to do with her getting picked. Instead, she was told that it came down to a combination of intelligence, psychological testing, physical endurance, and desire. The clincher, however, was the fact that she had no family to speak of.

The higher-ups in the Project knew that the chances of anyone making it home were slim at best, and their travelers didn't need the distraction of getting homesick. Whereas homesickness was always a possibility, it would reduce the longing if the travelers had no one waiting for them. So, adding "French" to the languages spoken section was an unnecessary fib.

And now, she was paying for her deception.

There were no hard and fast rules when it came to the

assignments. The project's primary purpose was to monitor how well the participants adapted physically, mentally, and emotionally to time travel. They were each given a rough agenda of places and times to visit. But it was understood by all that due to the portals' locations, the plan was only a suggestion. Simone could have skipped this part of the journey, and no one would have had a problem with it. And what if they did? Since she was a volunteer, it's not like they could dock her pay or put her on suspension.

No, she was totally on her own and in charge of her destiny.

So why the hell did she choose to visit France in 1813?

She was in hiding. The portal she accessed was in a rundown area of Paris in 1947. The destruction from the German bombings in the war was still all around her. Rebuilding was slow in coming.

However, Paris of 1813 was worse. Rats were everywhere, and everyone she saw seemed hungry. The portal brought her out between two tenements in a garbage-strewn alley. The first thing Simone noticed was the smell. It was the smell of death. Two dead rats were at her feet, but Simone knew that the smell came from something larger.

As she moved closer to the street, she saw it. Lying in amongst a pile of garbage was a body. She had no idea if it was male or female, but it didn't matter. It had been there a long time.

Simone moved farther down the alley. She had to find a hidden spot to check the Portal Finder. There had to be another portal in Paris, one that would take her ... well, anywhere.

There was one, but it wasn't in Paris. It was in the countryside about fifteen miles away. It was perfect. It would take her to 1960. From there, she'd find another portal to somewhere.

She looked down at her clothes. Definitely not Paris of 1813. She had forgotten to find out what they wore in 1813. That was a serious mistake. The purpose was to remain unnoticed. Simone put the Portal Finder in her backpack and quietly approached the alley entrance. She really didn't have to be quiet. The noise on the street, with loud wagons and people calling each other, more than covered any noise she might make.

Simone sat against the wall. She had to think for a minute. She had always done well in history and knew that something significant had happened in France around this time. The War of 1812? No, that was in America. Something else.

Napoleon! He invaded Russia in 1812 and suffered a massive defeat. Did the people know that yet? Did she land in 1813 or 1812? Portals weren't always reliable. She checked the Portal Finder. It was 1813. If they knew of Napoleon's loss, conditions wouldn't be stable. Would there be anger? Had it affected the economy of France? She didn't remember learning about that. So much for history class.

Simone needed clothes so she could blend in. Maybe she could ask someone for clothes. What was the word for clothes? Vêtements? She'd give it a try.

She stepped out onto the street, and everyone around her stopped what they were doing and stared. It was as if the whole road had become frozen.

Simone walked over to a woman with two children cowering under her skirt.

"J'ai besoin de vêtements."

The woman just looked at her, not comprehending what Simone said.

"J'ai besoin de vêtements," she repeated.

The woman turned and ran.

People were now talking to her, but Simone didn't understand them. Was her French that bad? Probably. Did they speak a different dialect? Maybe. Either way, she didn't understand them. Plus, they were all speaking at once.

A soldier approached her and said something that she didn't

understand. He turned to another soldier and said something. The man must have agreed because each man took one of Simone's arms started walking with her. Where were they taking her? She tried to speak, but suddenly, she couldn't remember a word of French.

Would any of them know English?

"Does anyone speak English?"

That shocked the two men. They spoke among themselves, and Simone was pretty sure she heard the word "English." Suddenly, the men weren't quite as gentle with her. They walked for about fifteen minutes before arriving at a dark wall. Beyond the wall was an equally dark building. Simone couldn't see any movement. They walked along the wall until they reached an iron gate. One of the men rang a large bell situated next to the door.

Simone suddenly saw her chance and pulled away from the men. She broke their grip and started to run. Behind her, she heard one of the men call out. She couldn't hear what he said, but she took a quick look over her shoulder. The soldier was pointing a pistol at her.

She stopped. The two men ran to her and grabbed her, roughly leading her back to the gate. A man had appeared on the other side of the gate by then. He began talking to the soldiers. Simone didn't understand a word of what was said, but the soldiers kept pointing at the clothes she was wearing. *So much for blending in,* she thought.

One of the soldiers grabbed her backpack and opened it.

"No. Please give it back."

They ignored her and the soldier pulled out the Portal Finder. The men had a long discussion about it before finally putting it back in the backpack and handing it to the man inside the gate. The man opened the gate, and the soldiers walked through, with Simone in tow.

They entered the building, and Simone knew exactly where

she was. A sense of despair overcame her.

She was in a lunatic asylum.

She screamed out that she didn't belong there and tried to pull away, but the men refused to let go. Finally, the man in charge called out to a pair of orderlies, and the men took her from the soldiers. The orderlies were disgusting men with bad teeth, greasy hair, and ripe body odor. Following the man's orders, they took Simone along a long hallway littered with babbling men and women until they reached a room with a dozen beds. The men talked and laughed the whole way while they pinched and fondled Simone.

She was terrified because she knew what was coming next.

One of the men produced a simple cloth dress and motioned her to take off her clothes. When she hesitated, the men forcibly ripped off her clothes. They pushed her onto the bed. One of the men held her down while the other violently raped her. Then they switched places. When they were finished, they threw her the dress and motioned for her to put it on.

Simone curled up in the corner of the bed and cried for hours. She was left alone until dinnertime when she was told to go to the dining room. She didn't want to go. She just wanted to stay where she was. She was in a lot of pain, and she felt sick to her stomach. She didn't want to move.

Simone was forced to move and was led to a large room with a dozen long tables. It was painful walking, and she felt shellshocked. Could her life get any worse?

She stood in line for a bowl of grayish substance with the consistency of oatmeal. Bugs were crawling on the side of the bowl. She was told to sit next to a young woman with a vacant stare. Simone wondered if her stare was just as vacant. The woman pulled her bowl of gruel closer to her body so that Simone wouldn't steal it.

Simone looked around. The room held about two dozen

inmates of both sexes. Some were babbling in French, and others, like her neighbor at the table, didn't say a word.

She tried her best to focus on her situation, and not on what had been done to her. *Think!* She thought to herself. *There must be a way out.* But today was not the day for it. She was depressed, she had been violated, and she couldn't communicate with anyone. Most of all, she didn't know why she was there. Yes, she did. When she showed up wearing strange clothing and not speaking French, it scared people. The easiest option for the soldiers was to take her to the asylum and let them deal with her. Was this the result? Was she going to eventually talk to someone in charge?

Things didn't improve over the next few weeks. Other than being raped by the orderlies at their whim, she was left alone to wander. She learned quickly that all of the younger women faced the same fate as she did with the orderlies, especially the girl she ended up eating next to every day. However, as much as she tried, she couldn't get the girl to talk to her. Not that it would have mattered, as Simone's French was almost nonexistent.

Simone knew that if she dwelled on the violence the guards were heaping on her, she'd go mad. She couldn't allow that to happen. So, Simone spent much of her time scoping out the building and possible escape routes. However, she couldn't even think of escape until she knew where her Portal Finder was. She discovered it during her second week, when she finally met the administrator.

The orderlies escorted her to his office. The man spoke rudimentary English. While not a cruel man, he was someone in a position he cared little about. As a result, he didn't want to concern himself with Simone's situation. Simone learned that she was at a state-run asylum and would remain there until cured. Cured of what, she didn't know. She couldn't get him to understand any explanation she gave him. He did, however, show an interest in the Portal Finder.

He picked up the Portal Finder from his desk and asked her about it. What could she say? She turned it on, hoping the flashing lights would scare him. It worked. The lights terrified him so much he made her turn it off, and put it in the backpack, which he put it on the floor in the corner of his office. The office had a door leading outside. If only she could overpower the man, maybe she could escape. But he was a large man, and she would never be able to subdue him.

While many of the inmates were demonstrably insane, a couple were in similar situations as herself—having no idea why they were there or being imprisoned there falsely. One of the men knew a few words of English. With that tenuous connection, Simone improved her French enough to have conversations.

Jean-Paul was an older man who was once a schoolteacher. He ended up at the asylum five years earlier based on something insulting he had said to a government official. The official could have had Jean-Paul put to death or sent to one of the many French prisons. But he had a perverse sense of humor and assigned him to the asylum. Jean-Paul informed Simone that escape was impossible. She refused to believe him, but as time went on and her plans of escape were met with failure, she began to realize that he was right.

Her friendship with Jean-Paul was a glimmer of light in a horrible situation, but that ended about four years into her stay when he simply disappeared one morning. She never found out what happened to him.

Occasionally, Simone would fight with one of the orderlies, landing her in solitary confinement. She looked forward to these times, as the orderlies would leave her alone. As time went on, she started more fights with orderlies so they would send her to isolation. She was always taken to the administrator after one of these events, and each time, she saw her backpack with the Portal Finder gathering dust in the corner. So there was always hope....

Simone's chance for escape came in her eighth year in the asylum. They had changed administrators, and the current one was an alcoholic. She'd had another fight with an orderly and was taken to the administrator after doing her ten days in isolation. This day, the administrator was almost incoherent. For the first time in years, Simone saw her chance at escape.

The man became amorous in his drunken state, so Simone let him and even encouraged it. She removed her drab gray dress and let the man see what was under it. In his excitement, he got stuck trying to take off his pants. While he concentrated on his problem, Simone picked up a paperweight from his desk and struck him in the head. He fell to the floor, and with the man's blood pooling up around his head, Simone picked up the dusty backpack, making sure the Portal Finder was still inside, and carefully opened the door that led outside. There was no one there. She made it to the outer gate without being seen and headed to the closest portal. On the way, she stole clothes from clotheslines to make her look more presentable if she encountered someone on her way to the portal.

A few hours later, she was standing in front of the portal.

After eight years, she was finally free!

*****

"For eight years, I was raped several times a month. I had five miscarriages over the years."

Hal thought he was going to throw up. He didn't know what to say.

Finally, with a crack in his voice, he asked, "Any children?"

"They wouldn't have allowed that. Three of the miscarriages were intentional on their part. They beat me until I miscarried."

"I'm so sorry. I don't even know how to respond to all that."

Hal put his hand on hers to show support, but she pulled it away.

"I'm sorry," she said. "I know you are just being kind, but I can't have anyone touch me. Not now. Do you know what's sad? Well, one of the many sad things? Once upon a time, I enjoyed sex. I can't imagine ever having a man touch me again in that way. When I think of all the men who raped me, I get physically sick."

"My friend, Ray, said that people had heard that you weren't doing well, and when they didn't hear from you, they thought you might have committed suicide."

"I can't say I didn't try. Once I tried to hang myself, but they caught me in time, then whipped me. Whipping me was another favorite pastime."

She turned her back to Hal and lifted her shirt.

"Oh my God!" he said. Her back was a mass of red welts and scars.

She dropped her shirt and turned around. Hal's face told the whole story.

"I'm sorry to show you that," she said.

"No, it's okay," he replied. "It just tells me what an amazing woman you are to have dealt with all that for so many years. Anyone else would have cracked in a matter of days."

"I can understand why my colleagues thought I wasn't doing well. I was homesick and had expressed it in some of my reports. And then I fell off the grid. They couldn't have known about the asylum."

To get her into a different frame of mind, Hal asked, "Where did you go from there?"

"I found the portal near Paris, and it led me to now—1960. I had heard about this house from a report and decided to head over here to rest. A trucker took me to the coast, and I snuck my way aboard a ferry. I've only been here a day, looking over my shoulder the whole time."

Hal noticed her shaking as she talked. Whatever they had done to her had affected her whole nervous system.

"I don't know if the shaking will ever go away," she said, sensing his thoughts.

"You need some time *not* looking over your shoulder," he said. "I think you should go in the bathroom and run a hot bath. You should then soak in that bath for as long as you want. Not that you need it with me, but the bathroom door has a lock if it will make you feel better."

Hal saw the makings of a smile.

"Thank you," she said. "I haven't had a real bath in years. I will take you up on your offer."

"Tomorrow, when the stores open, I will buy you a couple of outfits, so you can wear something new and clean."

Minutes later, Hal heard the bath running. He felt tired enough to sleep but felt he owed it to Simone to stay awake and stand guard.

Tomorrow, they could discuss the next steps.

Chapter 36

Hal was dozing off when Simone came out of the bathroom. Hal looked at his watch. She had been in there for over two hours and looked like a new woman. She had on a robe that Hal had left for her. Although still damp, her hair had lost its wildness. Her face was bright, though still lined and tired and bruised. The heaviness surrounding her, while not gone, had lightened somewhat.

"I'm sorry," she said when she saw him stretching. "You stayed awake for me. If I'd known, I would have finished sooner."

"I didn't want you to finish sooner. I'm glad you took your time. I prepared the guest room for you."

He stood up and led her into her bedroom. He had made the bed and had put a glass of water on the bedstand.

"You've been so kind to me," she said. "I don't know how to thank you."

"Someone needs to be kind to you. The only way you can thank me is to try to put the last eight years behind you. But I know it won't be easy."

"Impossible is more the word, but I understand what you are saying. I'll never be able to forget it, but maybe over time, it will begin to fade."

She didn't look confident that it would ever happen.

"What are your plans?" she asked.

"Ray and Natalie, along with your friend Hanna and her

friend Alex, went to Australia. There's a portal there that goes back to 1901. Ray left me a note telling me where they were going, so I planned to join them. I'd love it if you accompanied me."

"I was going to ask if I could, so thank you."

Simone talked calmly, but Hal could see her shaking. Would that ever go away?

*****

The next morning, Hal was up early and went to a nearby bakery for croissants, scones, and muffins. He didn't know what Simone liked, so he thought an assortment would do the trick. He was making coffee when Simone emerged from the bedroom. She wore the same outfit she had the day before, but everything else had changed. Her hair was clean and brushed, and her face displayed the makings of a smile.

"Good morning," said Hal.

"Good morning. That coffee smells wonderful. Who would have known that something as simple as coffee could excite me? The pastries look so good, too. And I had my first restful night's sleep in I don't know how long."

"I'm glad. After breakfast, we can get you some clothes. You'd probably like a haircut, too."

"I don't have any money," said Simone.

"It seems that Ray anticipated my arrival," said Hal. "Last night, I found an envelope in one of the kitchen drawers with my name on it. There was enough money in it to take care of these little things, as well as enough to get us to Australia. We just have to figure out how to get there. We have no passports. Maybe with all of your time traveling experience, you can suggest something."

"Ha! Time-traveling experience? You forget that I started twelve years ago but spent the last eight years otherwise occupied."

Hal found the fact that she worded it with a bit of humor encouraging.

"I only went to a few places before my disastrous decision, so I'm not much more experienced than you."

"Okay, then we'll put our heads together and come up with something. Unfortunately, I doubt if we could find someone to create fake passports. And it would probably cost us too much," said Hal.

"And risk being thrown in prison," added Simone. "I couldn't take that again." She shivered as she said it.

"I had to escape the States covertly," said Hal. "I knew someone who smuggled me aboard a cargo ship. Maybe we could use some of the money to bribe our way onto one."

"Or see if we could work for passage," suggested Simone.

They ate their breakfast in comfortable silence with those ideas to consider, then ran their errands. By early afternoon, Simone had new clothes and had her hair done. She had it cut short, explaining that it made her feel free. Hal realized that he needed some 1960-appropriate clothes, as well.

"Where are we going in Australia?" asked Simone.

"The best I can determine from the Portal Finder is that it's somewhere in the desert."

"Great."

Hal laughed.

"Hey, I'm not complaining," said Simone. "I'm free. That's all that matters."

Without warning, she burst into tears. Hal was frozen, not sure what to do. She had already made it clear that she didn't want to be touched. He grabbed a dishrag and handed it to her. She nodded in thanks and wiped her face as the tears flowed. After a couple of minutes, she lowered the dishrag and gave Hal a faint smile.

"Thank you. That just appeared out of nowhere."

"Well, not exactly nowhere," said Hal, "and I'm sure it won't be the first."

"Thank you for understanding."

They bought fish and chips for dinner and decided that it was time to leave. They would take the train to London the following day. Both were anxious to be on their way.

*****

Hal was awakened that night by a noise in his bedroom. He opened his eyes to find a man in a black beard staring down at him. In the man's hand was an object that looked like a weapon. The man spoke.

"You are not supposed to be here."

Chapter 37

"Wh-what?"

Was he dreaming?

"You are not supposed to be here." The man raised the weapon. "I'm sorry."

Hal moved quickly, and a hole appeared in his pillow. The weapon made a strange popping sound.

He dropped to the floor as another shot put a hole in the mattress. His back was against the wall, so he pushed on the bed with his legs. The bed hit the man in the knee, and he cried out. He shot, putting a hole in the wall next to Hal.

Hal was fighting for his life. He grabbed his pillow and flung it at the man. It hit the gun arm, moving it slightly, and the man's next shot went wild. The man aimed the gun again. Then Hal caught a movement in the doorway. It was Simone.

She reached the man, and as he began to turn, she shoved a kitchen knife into his back. He cried out and sank to his knees. Hal jumped up and kicked the weapon from the man's hand, then kicked the man in the head. He needn't have bothered. The man was already dead. He fell face-first to the floor.

Hal was breathing heavily. He sat on the bed, and Simone grabbed him by the arm in concern.

"Are you okay? Are you shot?"

"No, I think I'm okay. Thank you. You saved my life."

"You saved mine," Simone said quietly.

She moved to hug Hal, then backed away before she could follow through.

"I've never seen a weapon like that," Hal said, pretending not to notice her movements.

"I have," said Simone. "I've used one. It's from where I come from, which means that this man was from my time, as well. But why? I don't recognize him."

"He told me I wasn't supposed to be here," said Hal. "Then, before he pulled the trigger, he told me he was sorry. What does it mean?"

"I don't know. He wasn't part of my group, but why is he here?"

"He was coming after me, specifically," said Hal. "Ray mentioned something about them sending assassins back to kill anyone who went through a portal unofficially."

"'Unofficially.' That's a good one," said Simone. "Technically, we've all gone through unofficially. Who's official? But now we know that someone is after you."

"And maybe you, too."

"Wonderful," she said quietly.

"It seems that someone is after me no matter what decade I'm in," said Hal, shaking his head. "I can't seem to escape it. And now I have to clean up another body. When I was hiding the other bodies in the shed back in 2023, I tripped over a bone sticking out of the ground. I wonder if it was this guy. But then, he wasn't dead yet, or was he?"

He dragged the body into the backyard, confident that no one would see him in the middle of the night. He was going to dig where he had tripped but then noticed that the ground had already been dug up.

"I don't think I was responsible for the body here," he said to Simone. "I think this is Ray's work. Can you help me carry this guy? I want to take him far into the woods, but I don't want to leave drag marks."

The man was heavy, but together they took him about a hundred feet into the dense foliage. Hal checked the man for ID and found none.

"That's not unusual," said Simone. "They didn't want anyone time traveling with identification."

Since there was no way they would go back to sleep, they spent the rest of the night preparing for their trip. Simone showed Hal how the weapon worked and told him that it should always be kept on "stun" to avoid accidentally killing someone.

"So it doesn't take bullets?"

"No bullets. Bullets went the way of the dinosaurs in the last few years of the 20th Century. They are only used in antique guns now."

"I find that ironic," said Hal, "since I used to run a magazine that focused on antiques. Now I'm the antique who carries an antique gun. So, you never have to reload?"

"No."

"Interesting. Well, you carry that one, and I'll carry mine. I have a feeling we're going to need them."

They were on the early train to London a few hours later. As they left the house, Hal looked back at it with a sense of nostalgia. It was a strange situation that brought him to the house, but he had come to think of it as a second home.

"Do we have a plan?" Simone asked.

"I like your idea of signing on with a ship as crew," replied Hal. "Maybe we can find one that doesn't care about identification."

As soon as they arrived in London, they walked to the docks. It was a long walk, but they needed to save the little bit of money they had. They didn't know how long it would take to find someone willing to transport them.

There were no ships making an Australia run in the port, but they were told that two would be docking the next day. So, they found a fleabag hotel and rented a room. They weren't sure how long they were going to have to stay there, but as Hal looked around the hovel, he just hoped it wouldn't be long at all. He suddenly missed his nice clean condo outside Boston.

Luckily, the room had two beds. It would allow them to avoid any awkwardness. To conserve their meager bit of money, they bought cans of food and loaves of bread.

They were at the docks the next day when the ships came in. Knowing the crew would be busy unloading and loading freight, they observed and bided their time. Then, late in the day, they approached the first ship's captain and asked if he could take them to Australia. They explained that they had no money but would be willing to work for passage. The captain told them that they could buy passage but that he had no need for more crew.

The captain of the second ship gave them a similar answer.

By making friends with some of the longshoremen, they found out that Australia-bound ships would come in every day that week. They promised to pass the word that Hal and Simone were looking for passage. No one questioned why. Hal figured they had seen it all and had no need to ask.

Three days went by with no luck. They were almost out of money and would soon be homeless.

"We were taught that in extreme situations, we are allowed to break the law, as long as it affects as few people as possible. For example, we could rob a bank or a store," said Simone.

"Ray told me about that in one of his communications," said Hal. "He said that your friend Max had to rob a bank. I would rather not, but extreme situations call for extreme measures. Let's give it a bit more time."

They struck paydirt the next day. A scruffy sailor approached them as they sat at the edge of an empty boat slip.

"Word gets around that you're looking to work your way to Australia." The man had an American accent.

"American," said Hal. "We are, too."

"Detroit," said the man.

"Boston," replied Hal. "And yes, we need to get to Australia, but have no money...." He hesitated. "Or papers."

"That won't be an issue. Can you cook? We lost a couple of our kitchen staff when we arrived. Took off the minute they got on shore."

"I was a cook in a restaurant in my youth," replied Hal, lying through his teeth. He wasn't sure the guy believed him, but it didn't seem to matter.

"I'm Walt," said the man.

"Hal and Simone."

"Well, Hal and Simone, it won't be easy. Eighteen-hour days. The head cook is an asshole. The only fresh air you'll get is when you go off duty at night or dump food over the side. Not easy, but you'll get to Australia in about forty days. Want the job?"

"We'll take it," said Hal. "And Walt, thanks."

"Save it. By the end of the trip, you might not want to thank me. Do you need to get your belongings?"

Hal and Simone held up their backpacks.

"Everything is here," said Simone.

"Then follow me."

Hal knew where the term "rust bucket" came from when they saw the ship. It was an old freighter with fading paint and more rust than he'd ever seen.

"All surface rust," said Walt, reading his thoughts. "The old girl runs great."

They climbed the gangplank. When they reached the deck, Walt told the captain that he'd found the kitchen replacements. The captain distractedly welcomed them aboard.

"He's busy right now," said Walt, "but you'll see him at

meals."

"How many crew members?" asked Hal.

"Thirty-two," answered Walt.

He showed them to their cabin, a room not much larger than a closet. It had one single bed.

"I'll sleep on the floor," said Hal.

"We can take turns," said Simone.

"No, I'm fine. I've slept on many a floor in my life. Besides," he said with a chuckle, "it looks more comfortable than the bed."

They were put right to work. Walt took them down to the galley, where they met Liam, a crusty Irishman with a glued-on sour expression. He put Hal on dishwashing duty—the former galley crew took off before finishing their morning chores. He had Simone peel potatoes.

When the crew showed up for supper, a few of them gave Simone a lusty look.

Hal knew at that moment that it was going to be a trouble-filled voyage.

Chapter 38

That night, once they were off duty, Hal and Simone stood on the deck looking out at the night sky. It was chilly, and Walt had managed to rustle up a couple of grease-stained sweatshirts for them.

"It's going to take us 40 days to get Australia," said Hal. "I hope that we will still be able to go through the portal and hook up with Ray."

"It doesn't matter how long it takes us," said Simone. "Time doesn't matter. We could spend a year getting to Australia and go through the portal and still end up getting there before Ray. That's the nice thing about time travel. You are never late or early for anything."

Hal laughed. "I'll never understand it."

"Nobody understands it," said Simone. "That's one reason we were sent out on this project. But I don't think it will ever be completely understood."

The first week went relatively peacefully. Liam was a taskmaster but not unkind. The work was hard, starting early in the morning and lasting well into the evening. A few of the crewmembers made lewd comments to Simone, and when the captain was around, he stopped it. But he was rarely in the galley, often preferring to eat in his room. Hal couldn't blame him. The dining room was a spartan place.

Hal kept his gun in his backpack, but he insisted that Simone keep her weapon in her belt as a precaution. She wore baggy clothes to cover it up. Then, halfway through the voyage, she had to use it.

One of the sailors, nicknamed Squiggy, had been on Simone's case from the beginning. She and Hal knew that it would lead to trouble, but they were just hoping to get through the trip without Squiggy escalating.

It was late in the evening, and Hal was on deck dumping the food scraps. Liam had left the kitchen an hour earlier, so Simone was alone. Squiggy must have been watching for the opportunity because he arrived the moment she was left alone.

"Hi, darlin'." Squiggy was from Texas and one of three American members of the crew. "I have you all to myself."

Squiggy didn't scare Simone. After everything she had gone through, very little would ever scare her again.

"Please leave me alone," she said, knowing it would be ignored. But Squiggy hadn't waited all this time to back off at a simple request.

"Ah, darlin', you don't mean that. We were made for each other. Let me show you a little lovin'. How come you shake so much? I always see you shaking. Are you scared?"

He had been inching closer and now grabbed her forcefully, pulling her toward him. He pushed her against the wall and kissed her, his hands roaming freely across her body. She pushed him, but that only made him more aggressive. He was rough now and was trying to undo her jeans.

She reached behind her back and grasped her weapon tightly. She brought it up and pushed him until he was about a foot away. She pulled the trigger, and Squiggy slammed against a table, sinking into a sitting position. He was unconscious.

Hal walked in at the moment she pulled the trigger.

"Are you okay?"

"I am. He's been better."

"Now I know what the stun setting does," said Hal. "Did he see the weapon?"

"No, he couldn't have."

"Good. Give it to me so that you don't have any weapons on you. I will put it away with our things when I get a minute. We'll let Squiggy forever wonder how you got the best of him."

Simone smiled, but Hal could see some tears, and her shaking had increased. He figured it must have triggered flashbacks of her eight years locked away. But there was little he could do to help. Simone had made it clear that if she was ever going to heal from her nightmare, it would come in its own time.

They contacted the captain, who was none too pleased to have his sleep interrupted. Soon, a group of sailors stood around Squiggy, who was still unconscious.

The captain said to Hal, "Are you telling me that you had nothing to do with this? She did this on her own?"

"I came in just after it happened. But I know that Squiggy has been giving Simone a hard time from the very beginning of the voyage."

"How did you do it?" asked the captain.

"My little secret," said Simone.

"Take him to the brig," said the captain. "He'll stay there till we dock." He turned to Simone. "Do you want to press charges?"

"No, I'd rather just forget it."

Simone was left alone from that point on.

They docked in Fremantle on the 40th day of their journey. Hal had never been so happy to see land. They said goodbye to the crew and thanked Walt. Although he was under no obligation, the captain gave them some money.

"You did a good job," he said. And to Simone, he added, "and I apologize again for your encounter with Squiggy. I won't turn him over to the police, but I'm docking his full pay for that sailing, and I'm giving it to you."

"That's not necessary," said Simone, "but it is appreciated."

A few minutes later, away from the ship, they counted it. It would be enough to buy a cheap car and some camping supplies.

Hal had a feeling that where they were going, they'd need it.

Chapter 39

FLAGSTAFF, ARIZONA—1959

From her bus window, Millie saw the lights of Flagstaff and knew she had made the right decision. After leaving the group in Saxmundham, she thought about her options and remembered Ray and Natalie talking about the portal at Hollow Rock, Arizona. She looked at her Portal Finder and saw that the Hollow Rock portal was still open. That was a much better choice than Australia. The Australia portal was in the middle of the desert. She would never survive that. Hollow Rock, however, was a town in 1870. From there, she could access almost anywhere in the United States.

But what would she do if she arrived when Ray and Natalie were still there? Hey, that wasn't her problem. They wouldn't know her. After a few days in Hollow Rock, she would take the stagecoach to San Francisco, St. Louis, or New Orleans. That would be quite the experience.

She caught a flight from London to New York. She saw the sights of New York for a few days and then took a flight from New York to Phoenix. In Phoenix, she caught a bus to Flagstaff. And that's where she was now, about to arrive in Flagstaff.

Millie knew the names of all the travelers who had gone through Hollow Rock and could be on the lookout for them. It would be interesting to meet fellow travelers. And since they didn't know Millie, she could make up any story about herself that she wanted.

She spent the next two days preparing for her trip through the portal, buying the right clothes for the time and visiting coin shops to buy currency. Finally, she was ready.

Millie took a taxi out to the site of the old town. The taxi driver asked if she was comfortable being left out there on her own, but she assured him that she knew what she was doing. He reluctantly dropped her off and headed back to Flagstaff. She could see him glancing at her through his rearview mirror as he drove away.

It took Millie over an hour to find the cave. The ledge leading to the cave entrance was narrow, and she had to be careful not to slip. When she reached the entrance, she called into the cave, hoping to scare any residents away, but she heard no sounds. So, she slowly crawled through the opening using her flashlight to look for unwanted animals. When she was sure she was alone, she stood up and looked around.

How strange to be in the same cave visited by Natalie in 2009 and Ray in 2021. She looked to see if the trunk found by Ray was there. She wouldn't open it, of course. She wouldn't want to interfere with events that had already happened.

It wasn't there. That was interesting. If she was more curious, she would have tried to figure out the physics of Ray not finding it until 2021, but it not being there now. Was it because Ray was now traveling, so the event had already happened even though 2021 was still 62 years away? But she only gave it a cursory thought. When it was all said and done, Millie really didn't care.

Using the Portal Finder as a guide, she found the narrow entrance to the portal. She took a deep breath to calm herself, then stepped through.

She suddenly heard the sounds of the town. She had made it!

She couldn't wait to see the old west. Millie left the portal entrance and crawled through the cave opening. There was the town below her! Now, the question was whether Ray and Natalie were there. What would she do if they were? Her best bet would be to stay under the radar and not draw attention to herself.

Millie carefully climbed down the hill from the cave and walked toward the town. It was cold! It looked to be close to winter. The question was, what year? She put on the coat she had bought just in case, then looked down at the Portal Finder in her hand. December 2, 1870. Well, that explained the cold.

She entered the town. It was a bustling place. She thought of Agnes and how her sister would have loved this adventure. She felt a momentary sense of guilt for abandoning Agnes, but there was so little she could do for her now. And then she thought of Jane, the friend they had stolen the original Portal Finder from. How had their actions affected her life? Again, the guilt crept in. She put it out of her mind. Hey, what was done was done.

"Where'd you come from?"

A young man with a badge on his chest was addressing her.

Where had she come from? Think fast.

"Uh, my horse died a few miles back, and I had to walk."

"In this cold?" asked the man incredulously. "It's a wonder you're still alive. In fact, you don't look like you've been walking far at all."

Millie had to change the subject fast. "I'm looking for my friends, Ray and Natalie." *What last names did they use?*

"We had a Natalie who worked at the saloon," said the marshal. *Or was he a sheriff? She didn't know.*

She shouldn't have used their names, but she had panicked. Millie was beginning to wonder if she was prepared for this after all.

"A guy showed up," said the marshal. "His name mighta been Ray. I don't know. He took her away. They left by stage two weeks ago. Some mighty sad fellers around here when she left. Hey, your name wouldn't be Millie, would it?"

"Uh, yes."

"A man is looking for you. Showed up about a week ago. A big guy. Said he was looking for an older lady—no disrespect intended—who hadn't arrived yet. Said her name was Millie."

Who would be looking for her here? It could only be someone who followed her through the portal but ended up arriving before her.

An assassin! That's all it could be.

"Oh no," she said, trying to will some tears to come. She had to have the marshal on her side. "If it's who I think it is, he's trying to kill me. You have to protect me."

"Why is he trying to kill you?"

"My husband owed him money," said Millie. "He killed my husband, and now he is after me."

"If I see him, I will detain him, but I can't arrest him just on your say so. If I find him, I will let you know, and then we can all have a sit-down. Will you be staying at the hotel?"

"I will. I'll go check in now. Please don't tell him I'm here."

That seriously complicated matters. If Ray and Natalie were gone, that meant there were no other travelers there from the first group. Ray and Natalie were the last to leave Hollow Rock. She had to leave now. She would take the next stage out of town. It didn't matter where it was going. She had to be on it.

She asked someone where the stage station was and was directed to a building down the street. When she got there, she saw that the next stage wasn't leaving for two days. Could she stay hidden for that long?

Millie went to the hotel and checked in. She was hungry. The hotel had a restaurant, but could she chance it? She'd have to. She had a feeling she'd be able to pick out the assassin pretty fast. No matter how hard they tried, people from the future never seemed to fit in.

Millie went downstairs and ordered beef stew at the restaurant. It was delicious and it filled her up quickly. When she was finished, she hurried back to her room. She hadn't seen anyone who fit the description of the assassin.

The marshal stopped by the next day to say that he hadn't seen the man who was looking for her.

"He mighta visited another town while he waited," said the marshal. "I'll keep my eye out."

Millie went back to the restaurant the day the marshal stopped by, figuring it might be safe if the assassin was out of town. And right after she ate, she was back in her room.

Millie was going stir crazy. She was in Hollow Rock and wanted to see the town, but it was impossible with the assassin out there. She felt trapped. Well, she wasn't going to wait around and live the rest of her life in fear. She was going to experience the old west. She didn't even know that it was an assassin looking for her. Maybe it was someone else from the future.

She left her hotel room with a determination she hadn't felt in a long time. She would soak up Hollow Rock and then catch the stage tomorrow to St. Louis. From there? Who knows?

She didn't even get to the end of the hall. The door to one of the rooms opened, and a large man stepped out. He looked up and down the hall and then said, "Millie?"

Millie stopped and let out a little cry.

"You aren't supposed to be here," said the man.

"I'm sorry," said Millie. "I'm an old lady. Please let me live out the rest of my life."

As she said it, she knew he wouldn't. A jumble of thoughts went through her head. Agnes … Jane … Alex and Hanna….

She never heard the shot. Instead, she felt intense pain, then nothing.

Millie was buried the next day with a simple wooden grave

marker and message.

Millie
Shot December 3, 1870.
No one knew her

Chapter 40

WESTERN AUSTRALIA—1960

It took Hal and Simone two days to find the Australian portal. First, they bought a cheap used car in Perth for cash, then stole a license plate to make the vehicle appear legal. Next, they purchased camping equipment, food, and water. They also loaded the car with filled gas cans, not knowing how many gas stations they would pass.

Hal knew that their destination was in desert country, so he just hoped that the clunker car would make it. They had passed through a few small towns, but this section of Australia was remote.

"You know," said Simone, "when we go through the portal, we'll end up around 1901. So how are we going to get back to civilization? And how do we know that your friend will be waiting for us?"

"Maybe we'll be waiting for him," said Hal.

"Good point, but the same problem."

"I think we should carry as much of this camping gear, food, and water as we can," said Hal.

"We have to make sure we are connected when we go through the portal, or we'll end up getting there at different times."

"Good to know. As for transportation, I guess we just wing it. Do you know where we're going?" he asked.

"The Portal Finder is pinpointing it a little bit more. It's near a place called Neale Junction."

Hal looked at the map.

"I hope you're joking."

"Sadly, no."

"Neale Junction is in the middle of nowhere—*really* in the middle of nowhere."

"Great. I had a feeling...."

"Can we drive a car through a portal?" asked Hal.

"I imagine you can, but I've never heard of a portal that large. Besides, it goes against every rule of time travel. If someone found this, it could seriously change history."

"Just a thought. I wonder why Ray chose this location?"

"I can tell you that. Unfortunately, this era doesn't have a lot of portals, and most of them are in locations we don't want to visit. I wondered the same thing myself last night and looked it up on the Portal Finder. He didn't have a lot of choices."

"Well, if he made it there before us, I hope he left a note," said Hal. "If not, we'll leave a note for him and start walking back to Perth. Do you wonder if this is going to be a big mistake?"

"It has crossed my mind. But then, after the last eight years, it's all freedom to me."

From time to time, Hal glanced over at Simone and wondered what thoughts were going through her head. From a real-time perspective, it had been less than two months since her escape from the asylum. That wasn't long enough to heal. Was healing even an option? Her encounter with Squiggy hadn't seemed to affect her adversely, but was it all an act on his behalf so he wouldn't worry? The asylum had done some real damage to Simone, both physically and emotionally. The tremors were constant, and it wasn't just her arms. Sharing the cabin on the ship had revealed other things. She often cried out in her sleep, and she tossed and turned all night. She had an eye twitch that Hal hadn't noticed at first. All in all, Simone was a mess. And yet, somehow, she was holding it together.

"What are you looking at?"

She was awake and saw Hal staring at her.

"You," he said. "I was admiring your strength and your ability to keep it all together. I would have never been able to."

"Bullshit."

"Bullshit?"

"Yeah, bullshit. Not all that long ago, you had a sedate life. You had a business to run and a nice home. And then your life exploded. You learned about the reality of time travel. You were hunted and almost killed several times, and then you went through a time portal knowing that you would never go home again. Now you are about to go through another one to a foreign time in a foreign country in the middle of the desert. I think you're handling it just fine."

"I hadn't thought of it like that."

"And for your information, I'm not strong. I'm hanging on by a thread."

"It's my turn to say bullshit," replied Hal. "I don't doubt that you are on the edge, but you went through an experience that few people in the world have lived through. It has broken you in many ways, but you are still here. So give yourself some credit."

The tears came, and Simone's body began to shake. Hal stopped the car and pulled her to him. She was sobbing now and finally letting out some of the demons that had inhabited her for so long. The fact that she was even letting him hold her was a significant step forward.

It lasted for many minutes. When she was done, she pulled away and leaned against her door, not saying anything. Finally, she whispered, "Thank you."

Hal didn't start the car moving until he felt she was ready to continue. After that, she was quiet for a while until finally coming out of it.

An hour later, the incident seemed to have been forgotten.

Hal left the road and drove across the desert when the portal became more clearly pinpointed.

"Coming up," said Simone. "Slow down."

Hal saw a parked car in the distance. A minute later, Simone had him stop next to the vehicle.

"It's right over there," she said, pointing to a large boulder. "It's right next to that rock."

"And I think we can assume that Ray and friends drove the car," said Hal. "So, they've been here."

They got out of the car and walked closer to the rock. Simone was watching the screen on the Portal Finder.

"Stop. It's right over there. It's five feet wide." She drew three lines in the sand to box off the entrance. As long as they didn't cross those lines, they'd be fine.

"Let's look for a note," said Hal. "I doubt if he left it in the car. He wouldn't have wanted anyone else to find it."

Hal was right. A search of the car yielded nothing. Then, a few minutes later, Hal found it in a protected spot between two rocks.

"Ray wrote it a few months ago," he said.

Hal, I don't know if you went through the portal back in Saxmundham and if you found my other note and the Portal Finder. If you are reading this, you did. We are about to go through this portal. As soon as we arrive in 1901, I will leave you another note. We will probably head for Perth and stay for a little while. Hopefully, we will see you there. Take care, Ray

"Now we know that they'll leave a note for us. If they are not there, we'll leave one for them and head to Perth," said Hal.

They gathered all their belongings and stuffed as much into the new large backpacks they bought—everything else they carried.

"Ready?" he asked.

"Ready."

They locked arms and went through.

PART FOUR

Chapter 41

NEALE JUNCTION, WESTERN AUSTRALIA—1901

"Australia in 1901 looks exactly like Australia in 1959," said Natalie jokingly. "If it weren't for the fact that our car is missing, I wouldn't have known that we'd gone through a portal."

"Does it remind you of when you went through the Hollow Rock portal?" I asked.

"Kind of. Except then, I had a town in the valley below me. There's nothing here."

We had flown to Perth and bought a car. The owner had some old license plates to give us on the sly, but when he found out we were heading for the desert, he told us not to worry.

"Once you get outside the city, no one will care whether you have plates or not," he said.

I had no idea what Hal's situation was. Had he seen the note hidden in the magazine? Was it a mistake to hide the message there? Had he found the money in the envelope in the kitchen drawer? Maybe all of this effort was moot. Maybe Hal never left the 21st Century. Maybe there was no one after him. Maybe they killed him—lots of maybes.

The chances were that I would never see Hal again. I knew that, but I had to try, though, just in case. There would have been nothing worse than for Hal to come through a portal to find himself all alone.

"Footprints," said Alex. "Two sets heading in the general direction of Perth."

I looked at Natalie questioningly. Hal, maybe?

"Someone came through the portal," said Hanna. "The footprints start here. There aren't any before this spot."

"Then, if it's Hal, he would have left a note," I said. I was excited. Could it be? But if it was, how long ago had he come through? I posed that question to Hanna and Nathan.

Hanna answered. "It's a strong portal," she said, "so the timeframe is condensed. If I had to guess, it couldn't have been more than six months, at the most."

"I agree," said Nathan. "But my guess is that it had to have been in the last few weeks … maybe days. It gets windy in the desert, and these footprints are still fresh."

"If it's Hal, who's with him?" asked Natalie. "Maybe it's just two people who came through by mistake. I know what that feels like."

"That's why we have to look for a note," I said. "Maybe it's in the same place I left one for him."

I looked over at the hiding place and saw the edge of a paper.

"I see it!" I yelled. I couldn't believe how excited I was. I ran to the spot and pulled the paper out from its hiding place.

The note read:

Hey, Ray. I'm with Simone, one of the original travelers.

"Tony was right. Simone is alive!" said Hanna. "I'm so happy."

We just came through the portal. The Portal Finder says it is October 1st, 1901. We have food and water. Hopefully enough to last us until we reach Perth. We will check into a hotel when we reach Perth and wait for you. We'll stay as long as we have to. Simone says hi to Hanna and can't wait to see her." ~ Hal

Hanna looked at her Portal Finder. "That was only two days ago. We're right behind them. Maybe we can catch them."

"Then we should leave now," said Alex.

"Are you looking forward to seeing Hal?" asked Natalie.

"I am," I said. "I'm also feeling guilty. I got him into this. If I hadn't told him about time travel, he'd still be living a normal life in Boston."

"We can't predict these things," said Hanna. "Besides, who's to say that he isn't having the time of his life? No pun intended."

We had no desire to stick around, so we headed out, following the footsteps of Hal and Simone.

It was hot. We tried our best to conserve water, but it wasn't easy. We ran across large rock formations and small groves of trees that provided us with shade, and we would take that time to rest. At one of the spots, we found the remains of a fire and some empty cans. Hal and Simone had been there.

The land wasn't hilly, but there were gullies. Maybe there was a rainy season in the desert?

At one point, two of the gullies intersected.

"Uh oh," I said. "Riders."

The earth was churned up by the passing of horses. I couldn't tell how many. Maybe a half dozen?

"It's fresh," said Alex. "Here are some horse droppings. Really fresh."

"They would have seen the footprints and followed. Hopefully, they are good people."

We found ourselves hurrying, feeling that Hal and Simone were close by. Then, a few minutes later, we heard voices—shouts. The riders had caught up to them.

"That doesn't sound good," I said.

The gully we were in emptied onto the plain. A few hundred feet farther was a scattering of large rocks. The riders were converging on one of the rocks where I assumed Hal and Simone were hiding.

There were five of them, and I could immediately tell these guys were scum. They might have been cowboys who worked at a local ranch. But more likely, they were just troublemakers. Their accents were thick, so I couldn't understand what they were saying. I didn't have to. Their tone and their gestures said it all.

Hanna said what we were all thinking.

"I don't care about the rules of time travel," she said. "These guys have to be dealt with." She pulled out her weapon. "I'm setting this on kill. Frankly, I'm getting tired of mean people. The fewer, the better."

"No arguments here," I said. I pulled out my Glock, and Nathan produced his weapon. Natalie pulled out the weapon we got from the dead assassin. I had once seen her shoot. She was good. Alex, the only one without a weapon, hung back.

We split up so we wouldn't be bunched together, and we came up behind the men.

I heard a shot, and one of the cowboys fell to the ground. That was Hal's gun.

The men became enraged and were about to charge when I shot one of them in the back. He landed on the ground but still moved, so I shot him again. I heard two pops of the futuristic weapons, and two more men went down. Another shot from the rocks, this time a pop, and the last man hit the ground dead.

It was over in a matter of seconds.

Hal and a woman I took to be Simone came out from behind the rocks. Simone and Hanna ran to each other and embraced. I approached Hal and held out my hand. The handshake turned into a hug.

"You're a sight for sore eyes," said Hal.

"You, too. Hal, this is Alex. He's from 1973. And this is Nathan. He's a former assassin from 2105. A long story. Over there is Hanna."

"And this is the famous Natalie," said Hal, giving her a hug.

"I've looked forward to meeting you," said Natalie.

Hanna and Simone approached the group, and introductions were made.

Getting rid of the riders was our first order of business. We found a hole in the gully that would fit all five bodies, and we covered them up with dirt. They would be found, but it might slow down the searchers. Then again, maybe no one cared enough to search for them. The horses were nowhere in sight. Before burying them, I went through the men's pockets and pulled out any cash they had. It wasn't a lot, but it might last us a few days in Perth.

We hiked a couple of miles farther, then camped for the night in the protection of a deep gully. Our campfire would be mostly hidden.

It was time we all got to know each other.

Chapter 42

It was a festive night, with a lot of catching up. Hanna and Simone spent some much-needed time together, speaking in hushed tones. At one point, I saw Hanna weeping and holding Simone tightly. However, it wasn't until later in the evening that I heard Simone's story and understood Hanna's emotion.

Most of our discussions were as a group, though, as we didn't want Nathan or Alex to feel out of place as old bonds were renewed. We took turns with our stories.

Hanna and Simone talked about the friendship they formed when training for the Project. By the time their training was completed, they had become like sisters. However, leaving on their journeys and knowing that they would probably never see each other again had been emotionally wrenching.

My heart went out to Simone when I heard her story. I could never imagine going through what she had suffered. The scars, emotionally and physically, were painfully apparent to us all. However, I had to give her so much credit for surviving the way she had. I noticed that she and Hal had developed quite a nice relationship, but based on her past and her pain, it would probably always be platonic.

Natalie and Hal hit it off immediately. That was to be expected, as I had talked to Natalie so much about Hal, and Hal was my sounding board when I was making my decision to travel back to Hollow Rock

Simone asked me to detail the deaths of her fellow travelers, "Uncle" Jim, Alan, and Max. Natalie provided the particulars of Herb's death at his lover's hands, the mystery author Beryl Dixon.

Hanna and Alex described their adventures during the Civil War and of meeting Millie. The subject of Millie was a sore spot for Hanna, so Alex did most of the talking.

"In the long run," said Alex, "Millie deceived us. There was a part of her that wasn't a good person. But there was also a part of her that I liked. She was feisty and unpredictable. And there was a kindness to her. Of course, she had her warts, just like the rest of us, but she also helped us out of a major jam."

"For her own purposes," added Hanna.

"Partly," responded Alex. "But I think she also really cared for us."

"I wonder what became of her?" I asked. "Did she go back to Atlanta or try to find a portal?"

"She wouldn't have come here," said Natalie. "She would have known that she'd never survive the desert. That would have been her only option."

"Or Hollow Rock," I said.

"Yikes," said Natalie. "That could complicate things."

"Well, if she had arrived before us, we'd remember seeing her, and I certainly don't remember her. So that makes me think that if she did go back, she arrived after we left."

"I vote that she went back to Atlanta to live out her days," said Hanna. "After all, she was 82."

The Millie talk ended there, but I did wonder what had happened to her after she left us. Maybe she stayed in England to take in the sights.

The two I felt for were Nathan and Alex. Nathan wasn't part of the group, even though everyone did what they could to include him. Like us, he had also been deceived, but his had resulted in the deaths of people. The Project hadn't been honest with him, and he could never forgive them for that.

I felt for Alex for a different reason. He came from the least technical era, and there was so much that we talked about that he couldn't relate to. Technology had advanced so far after 1973 that it was hard to explain it sometimes. He knew that, and I think it made him feel somewhat inferior or backward. However, the love between him and Hanna was genuine, and over time I was confident that she would bring him up to speed.

The next morning, it was time to plan. Over a breakfast of canned rations, we discussed our future. I started things off.

"I don't think anyone would disagree with me that we should stick together from this point on, right?" I asked. "After all, it took us long enough to find each other."

I got head nods from everyone.

"So, we have to ask ourselves what our ultimate goal is. Hal and Simone, we discussed all this back in England with no formal decision. Coming here was our decision. But what do we want to do beyond this? Going someplace where we are already alive in what I would call the 'alternate universe' would be difficult. That would eliminate the period from 1935, when Alex was born, through 2023, when Hal left Boston. And then the latter 20th Century, when Hanna, Simone, and Nathan were born, through about 2117, when Nathan was sent back. What does that leave us?"

"To arrive soon after 2023 would be one option," said Alex.

"Except that the NSA of that time is after Ray and me," said Hal.

"We could arrive after 2117," said Hanna, "but that presents problems, as well. First, the world is an ugly place and one that I was happy to leave."

"Amen," said Simone and Nathan almost simultaneously.

"Second," continued Hanna, "it is so advanced

technologically that all of you—Alex, Ray, Natalie, and Hal—would be overwhelmed by it. It would probably drive you insane."

She continued. "And third, to my knowledge, there is no portal that takes us that far ahead in time."

"Here's what I don't understand," said Alex. "We were all in England in 1959 or 1960. I was alive at that time, yet it didn't seem to affect anything. So, I was obviously in two places at once."

"I think we've proved that it can happen, but what are the long-term effects of that?" I asked. "But that's not the problem for me. Living in those times would be like repeating the past, in a sense," I said. "It's hard to explain."

"I get it," said Hal. "I was born in 1960. To go through the turbulent '60s all over again would be depressing. The Vietnam war, the assassinations of JFK, RFK, Martin Luthor King, and even John Lennon years later...."

"Wait a minute! John Lennon gets assassinated?" asked Alex with a shocked expression.

"He does," said Hal. "Besides experiencing all that, would we try in some ways to stop them from happening? It would be against the rules of time travel, but could we sit around knowing it was going to happen. And that only skims the surface. What about events in our own lives we'd try to prevent? My father was hit by a car and killed when I was twelve. Would I try to prevent that from happening?"

"And what if you did?" asked Hanna. "What other forces would it set into motion?"

"Exactly," said Hal.

"And that's why Natalie and I felt we couldn't stay in the house in Saxmundham," I said. "Well, one of the reasons."

"It seems to me," said Natalie, "that right now seems to be the best era for us. At least for now. Yes, historical things will always happen that we will be aware of, but they won't directly affect us.

The wars, the Depression, the Holocaust, are all things that will happen in the coming years, but they are events we have no control over. So maybe, for now, we are where we should be. If we don't like Perth, we can gather up some money and book rooms on a ship to America. Maybe we'd be more comfortable there."

"I wish I knew something about Perth in 1901," I said.

Natalie opened her backpack and produced a book.

"While you were negotiating for the car, I went into a bookstore and bought a book about the history of Perth. We have a long trip ahead of us, so we can read about it as we walk."

I looked around the group.

"So, let's get going."

Chapter 43

It took us many days to reach Perth. All of us—even Simone—were up to the grueling hike through the desert. Along the way, we learned some facts about the city, thanks to Natalie's invaluable purchase.

I was expecting a dusty little town with little to offer. But I was surprised to learn that Perth was modern for its day. Gold strikes in the region in the 1880s and 1890s had made Perth's population soar to almost 28,000. According to the book, 1901 was the last year of the gold rush, but by then, Perth had become a major city, with modern buildings, suburbs, and even an electric tram in the city's center.

We counted the money we had liberated from the dead cowboys and hoped that we had enough to cover four hotel rooms and meals for a few days. Even though the relationship between Hal and Simone wasn't sexual—to my knowledge, at least—the two had formed a strong bond and had become inseparable. So, sharing a hotel room wouldn't be an issue for them.

We entered the city of Perth in a driving rainstorm. In some ways, that was advantageous. The less attention we brought to ourselves, the better. I went into a store to ask where I could find a nice hotel. The store clerk told me that the best hotel in the city was the Palace, which had just been built. But as he looked me over in my muddy clothes, he suggested that I'd probably be happier at a smaller hotel at a less expensive price.

It was a good suggestion. We figured out that we could stay for almost a week and still have money for food. A week would give us enough time to get our bearings and figure out how to earn enough money to stay in Perth or take a steamship to America.

We took turns going to a church that distributed free clothes to the indigent. The church leaders took no note that we all had American accents—equal opportunity poverty.

The rain cleared up two days after we arrived. We all had appropriate clothing and felt comfortable roaming the city by then. We agreed to meet up for dinner and share our experiences.

At the end of the second day of roaming, Nathan—who had been walking the streets solo—had on a concerned expression as we met for dinner.

"Something happened to you," said Alex.

"Not to me, but there's something. It's just an impression," said Nathan. "But I don't think we're alone."

"In what way?" I asked.

"I think there are others of us here. Time travelers."

"Assassins?" asked Hanna.

"Not that I know of," said Nathan. "Let me explain what happened."

I looked around to make sure no one was listening.

"I was in a local watering hole sipping a beer. I figured what place is better than a bar for picking up information. I asked for another beer when a guy who had just sat down next to me asked me if I was a Yank. I said I was. Then he said something strange. He asked me if I was a part of the 'odd group.' That's the term he used. I told him I had just arrived in town yesterday and asked him what he meant by the 'odd group.' He said that it's a group of four Yanks who live on the other side of the city."

"Why are they odd?" asked Hanna.

"Rumor is that they just appeared one day—and I mean that in the literal sense. On the other side of town is a market that was crowded that day. There is a tiny cul-de-sac that someone was blocking with a booth. Suddenly, four people appeared in the cul-de-sac and had to squeeze past the booth. A dozen people saw them. They said that there was no other way they could have gotten into the cul-de-sac except the entrance that the booth was blocking. They also said they were dressed strangely."

"A portal?" I asked Hanna.

"No way. I've looked at the Portal Finder many times. There is no portal in Perth."

"I agree with Hanna," said Nathan. "I've looked as well."

"It's three men and a woman," said Nathan. "They are living outside the city in a cabin in the forest. They come into town for supplies. I guess they are tolerated because they spend money in the stores nearby. But, tolerated or not, people are scared. Some of the less-educated are calling them witches."

"They have money," said Natalie, "so they were prepared. That tells me that their arrival wasn't an accident."

The waitress brought our food, giving us time to digest the information.

When she was gone, I said, "So, they are American."

"Or maybe Canadian," said Alex.

"Right. Or Canadian. And they seem to have come through a portal, a portal not mapped on the Portal Finder."

I looked around the table.

"We need to talk to them."

Chapter 44

The next day was dark and rainy. Once again, the perfect weather to promote stealth. We split up into three groups, each group taking a different path to the meeting spot on the outskirts of Perth. Nathan accompanied Natalie and me.

"You're an experienced traveler," I said to him. "Is it possible that there are portals that the Portal Finder can't pick up?"

"I imagine so. Think of all the technological advances since your time. Take computers. At first, they were behemoths that filled an entire room. Then they developed the home computer. But these were extremely limited. As time went on, they became smaller and more powerful. They went through many more incarnations after that. The same thing happened to holographic technology, but most of that came after your time. So, who's to say that the Portal Finder wasn't given enhancements and made more powerful? Who's to say that there aren't thousands of portals that can now be tracked that we didn't know about before? We found out that there was another group after Hanna and Simone's group and after the eliminators like me were sent. By the time of the next group, the Portal Finder might have undergone a complete overhaul."

We were the last to reach the meeting point. There was a trail that led into the woods.

"How do we want to work this?" asked Hanna.

"We will probably scare them if we all go as a group," I said.

"I think two of us should go, with the rest of us close by in the woods," said Alex.

"I nominate Ray and Hanna," said Natalie. "If they are travelers, Hanna will be the best person to relate to them. And Ray is time tested in dealing with difficult situations."

Everyone seemed to agree to that, so Hanna and I started down the trail, with the others scattering into the woods and following. We had been told that the cabin was about a mile down the path, so it allowed me to get to know Hanna a bit better.

"Was any of this what you expected?" I asked.

"You mean the time travel in general?"

"Yes."

"No," she answered. "But you have to understand that we were trained by people who had no idea what they were talking about. All they could give us were generalities and suppositions. Not one of them had ever traveled before, so how could they prepare us for any of this? When I think back, I realize how shaky the foundation was. On the one hand, our whole mission was to determine the effects of time travel and provide those running the Project with our findings. But they spent weeks training us on … on what? A little bit of history, a lot of calisthenics to give us stamina, and a lot of rules of time travel. Who made up the rules?"

I laughed. "It sounds like most companies and governments," I said.

"Exactly. A bunch of self-important people telling others what they should do. You notice that none of them came with us."

"Would you do it again knowing what you know now?"

"That's difficult to answer," said Hanna. "On one hand, I never would have met and fallen in love with Alex. We've only known each other a short time, but already I can't imagine life without him."

"Natalie and I can relate to that."

"Right. So, for you, it was worth going through that portal, as it was for me. Emotionally, I would do it again. But taking Alex out of the equation, the answer is no. During the research for an unrelated project, the portals were discovered by accident. But they should have been left alone. Human nature, of course, wouldn't allow that. They had to investigate it, and I can understand that. But they never should have experimented with sending people through the portals. They were playing with fire, and they knew it. Where's it going to end? They were smart enough to put an end to it once, but then they started it up again."

"Desperation, maybe?" I asked. "They saw their world falling apart and felt they could find a solution in the past?"

"Desperation, yes. But mixed with arrogance. If they wanted to learn from the past, there were enough resources. But to think you could send people back to change the past? That's pure arrogance. And stupidity, I might add."

We saw the cabin ahead of us. There was smoke coming from the chimney. I touched my gun to make sure it was there and saw Hanna do the same.

"Here we go," I said quietly.

We arrived at the door, and I knocked. I heard movement from inside and voices talking softly. I couldn't hear what they were saying.

"Hello," I said when no one came to the door. "We're friendly."

"Who are you?" came a voice from behind the door. The accent was American.

"Fellow travelers," I said. "If you are who we think you are, you will understand those words."

"How do we know you aren't here to kill us?"

"A little paranoid?" I said quietly to Hanna.

"My name is Hanna Landers," Hanna said to them. "I was one of the original six. You may have heard my name. We are here with other travelers. We've come together because there is strength in numbers. There are assassins—they call themselves eliminators—who are out to kill us all. If we work together, we will all be a lot safer."

There was some more talking on the other side of the door, and finally, it opened, revealing four terrified people.

All I could deduce from first impressions was that meeting us would do wonders for them, but it would only impede our group. They were the sorriest collection of individuals I had ever seen. Maybe that was a slight exaggeration, but not by much.

There were four of them, three men and a woman. They all looked to be in their forties. The woman was slight, with dark, shoulder-length hair. One of the men was a big burly guy with blonde hair down to his shoulders in an unkempt mess. The second man was short, scrawny, and pale, about the palest person I had ever seen. He had Coke bottle glasses that made his eyes appear huge. The third man was the exact opposite of the second one. He was a tall, muscular black man with piercing dark eyes. Yet, despite their physical differences, they all had one common characteristic. Fear.

The woman seemed to be the spokesperson for the motley group.

"How can we believe you?" she asked.

"Well," said Hanna, "it doesn't look like you have a whole hell of a lot of choice in the matter."

The woman was silent for a moment, then said quietly, "You're right. Please come in."

"Our friends are out there. We'd like them to join us," I said.

The woman shrugged and gestured her acceptance. I called out to the others.

We were all standing in the cabin's living room a minute later. I introduced our group. Then the woman introduced their foursome.

"This is Doctor Simons," she said, indicating the burly guy. "This is Doctor Lind," she said, pointing to the pale guy, "and Doctor Wilson." The black guy gave a brief nod. "My name is Jane," the woman continued. "I'm not a doctor. More of a researcher."

"Are you from 2136?" asked Hanna.

"We are," came the answer. "And you and Simone are from the first group. We were given information about you before we left. We were told that the other four members involved in your mission are dead."

"They are," said Hanna.

"We didn't know about your mission until we met one of your associates," I said. "Her name is Millie."

"Associate?" Jane almost spat it out. "We didn't have an associate named Millie. If you met her, you met a fraud."

"I knew it," said Hanna. "I knew there was something wrong about her."

"Did you meet her sister, Agnes?"

"We did," said Alex. "They had been stuck in Atlanta for 40 years. They lost their Portal Finder...."

"MY Portal Finder," interrupted Jane.

"Millie is 82. We met Agnes, but she's older and has dementia."

"Good," said Jane. "And good that they were stuck there. It serves them right."

Jane proceeded to tell us a story about being picked for the Project and then robbed of her Portal Finder and research by her "friends," Agnes and Millie.

"I was lucky that they didn't kick me out of the program, but since they had already trained me, they gave me another chance. I hope Agnes and Millie burn in Hell."

None of the men had said anything. There was still fear in their eyes.

"Pardon my saying so," I said, "but you all seem terrified of something. Is there something we should know?"

"Yes," Jane answered.

"What?"

"You should be terrified, too!"

Chapter 45

"Terrified of what?" asked Natalie.

"Of everything," said Dr. Lind, the pale guy.

"Everything has fallen apart," said Jane. "Everything. We are the only four left from a group of twelve. That has given us reason to fear for our lives, but it's the least of the problems."

She suddenly realized that we were all still standing.

"I'm sorry for our rudeness. Please sit. I think we can find enough chairs for everyone."

After some shuffling, we were all seated, and Jane resumed her explanation.

"We received some communication before we arrived here, but I'm pretty sure it's the last we will get. Everything has fallen apart. The Time Travel Project, a resurrection of the original Project, has been infiltrated. They shut it down, but not before some unauthorized people stole Portal Finders and disappeared."

"The other thing," said Dr. Lind, "is that portals are closing by the hundreds, and they don't know why."

"Closing, as in disappearing?" asked Hanna.

"Yes."

"Which brings us to another question," I said. "A townsperson said that you showed up at the town market. It was a cul-de-sac, which means that it was the exit to a portal."

"Yes," said Jane.

"Our Portal Finder doesn't show a portal there."

"The new generation of Portal Finders are much more accurate and can pick up the energy trails of many more portals."

"What kinds of doctors are you?" asked Hal.

"As I said," answered Jane, "I'm a researcher."

"And the others?"

"I'm an anthropologist," said Simons.

"Biophysicist," said Lind.

"Biologist," answered Wilson.

"Someone is outside," said Alex, who had glanced out the window. "Two people. They don't look like locals."

Nathan went to the window.

"Eliminators. I can tell."

"What do we do?" asked Jane.

"They are not after you," said Nathan, "not if they are just going after unauthorized travelers."

"No," said Wilson. "They are going after everyone, just like you were trained in your day. They've closed down the Project again, and they have to eliminate everyone who went through a portal."

Nathan was silent for a moment, then said, "I'll see if I can talk to them."

Before we could react, Nathan opened the door and stepped into the clearing in front of the cabin.

"Hold your fire," we heard him say. "I'm one of you."

He made a showing of pulling out his weapon and laying it on the ground, then made a strange sort of hand signal. That must have done the trick. They told him to proceed, and he started walking toward the woods, where the men were hidden behind two trees.

That commenced almost an hour of waiting while Nathan talked to them. The two men did most of the talking, and we saw Nathan occasionally nod his head in agreement or understanding.

Finally, they all shook hands, and Nathan walked back to the house, picking up his weapon on the way.

When he entered the house, I referred to it being a long discussion.

"I learned a lot of things," he said. "Most of all, we've been lied to."

He lifted the weapon still in his hand shot each of the three men with Jane twice in the chest, six pops in rapid succession. He checked each body for signs of life. Then, satisfied that they were dead, he turned to face us. We all must have had shocked expressions.

"These men were no more doctors than I am."

He turned to Jane.

"You want to tell us the truth?"

"I did." Tears were pouring down her face.

"Not even close. These three were unauthorized. There wasn't a doctor among them. So, how much of what you told us is true?"

"I admit that those men were unauthorized. I didn't know it when I first met them. I didn't know until later. But all the rest of it is true," answered Jane. "The Time Travel Project is a mess."

"How do you know? You're not an official member of the Project anymore, so they wouldn't send you correspondence."

"No, but I know where most of the drop sites are. I read the incoming communications. It's true."

"But you are unauthorized, too," I said.

"Yes, but it's not fair. If it weren't for Agnes and Millie, I would be a valued member of the team."

"My heart goes out to you," Nathan said sarcastically.

"The other part that might not have been totally truthful was about us being the last living members of the second group. I have no idea of their status."

"Yeah," I said. "'Not totally truthful.' How about we call it a total lie?"

"Okay, I'm sorry. You have to understand. The people in that group were my friends. I trained with them. We lived together for several months until Agnes and Millie destroyed my dream. I care about the others, and I hope they are all okay, but I really have no idea."

She looked up at Nathan.

"Those people out there, the eliminators. I don't know how many they sent, but they were sent to hunt down unauthorized travelers, much in the same way you were. That means that I'm not the only one whose life is in danger. Most of your friends here are, as well. Maybe you can reason with them to let us live."

Even though it was just a popping noise, the shot made me jump. A hole appeared in Jane's forehead, and she slumped to the floor.

"You shouldn't be here," Nathan said sarcastically to her lifeless body.

I looked down at Jane, shocked that Nathan could so easily snuff out her life.

"She had to go," said Nathan. "She might have had the training, but she was as unauthorized as the other three."

"You still consider yourself an eliminator?" asked Natalie.

"No. They lied to me about my job, but it doesn't mean that none of it was true. These four were dangerous and had to be dealt with swiftly. The men out there filled me in on everything. Much of what she said was true. She was part of the group. Agnes and Millie did steal her information and Portal Finder. She was drunk, which was forbidden, and they kicked her out for it. The portal breach was a bad one. Over twenty unauthorized people went through. That concerned the heads of the Project, as it should have. Those twenty people stole six Portal Finders, so some are in groups like this one. They have one Portal Finder here."

"Which means Jane wasn't telling the truth about running

across the three men," I said. "If they only have one Portal Finder, they came through as a group."

"Exactly. As for the Time Travel Project, it is history, so to speak. They closed it down for good."

"They said that before, but it didn't stop them from resurrecting it," said Hanna.

"Supposedly, everything has been destroyed this time—equipment, documentation, and historical records. According to those guys, all traces of the Project are gone. The only issues are the authorized and unauthorized travelers. They all have to be eliminated. Numerous eliminators were sent back, but these guys don't know exactly how many. If they all do their job and eliminate the travelers, the only ones left will be the eliminators, and they all have MMD, like me, and will die out. Then, history will be clean, except for the occasional accidental traveler."

"They are eliminating all travelers?" I asked.

"Right, which means we now have to deal with our problem."

"Our problem?" Alex asked.

"The two eliminators out there. I made a deal with them that I would take care of these four in return for them leaving all of you alone. I'm fond of you all, and I trust you to do the right thing. But there is no way they will honor their end of the deal. They just used me to do part of their job for them. You are still targeted. Maybe I am too."

"We have to eliminate the eliminators," I said flatly.

"My job," said Nathan. "I'll do it. I'm a dead man walking. You are not. Wherever you go from here, you'll have a life. If I can kill them without dying myself, maybe I can share some of that life with you until it's my turn to die. If not, I will have done something worthwhile."

"We can all get them," I said.

"Only if I don't make it. If I don't make it, remember to take Jane's Portal Finder and the two from the eliminators. They are more advanced than yours, but mainly, we don't want the Portal Finders getting into the wrong hands. Oh, and Jane was telling the truth about portals closing down. The eliminators out there said the same thing. It's a phenomenon that no one can explain. What's showing as an active portal today might be gone tomorrow. Just keep it in mind if you plan to do more traveling."

Nathan held out his hand and we shook.

"Good luck," he said.

He slipped out the back window of the cabin.

I could have said that Nathan wasn't going to make it. It was almost like he had a premonition. A few minutes after climbing out the window, we heard a dozen or more pops, as well as some yelling. Then it went quiet.

We crept out the front door and scattered, just in case one of the eliminators was still alive. There was no need. The two were dead.

Nathan didn't die right away. He was bleeding profusely, and his breathing was ragged. There was no way we'd be able to stop the flow of blood. Natalie sat with him and put his head in her lap. She talked softly to him until he closed his eyes for good, and the breathing stopped.

We were all shedding tears. Nathan might have had the job as an eliminator, but he was a good person, and we would all miss him.

We weren't sure why, but we felt it important to bury him. We all said a few words and gave a moment of silence.

Then we got to work. We took all six bodies deep into the woods. If they had any clothes or other items that didn't fit 1901, we took them off the bodies. We burned everything in the fireplace and cleaned up any blood that was on the floor of the cabin. There would still be bloodstains, but no one would examine them closely. CSI didn't exist in 1901.

When we were satisfied that everything was in order, we

grabbed Jane's Portal Finder and the two from the Eliminators, as well as their weapons, and took the same routes back into the city that we had used earlier.

Chapter 46

We laid low for a few days, and even though we were staying in the same hotel, we chose to remain apart, being seen as couples and not as a large group.

We finally met a few nights later in a restaurant near the hotel to discuss our future. Between the dead eliminators and Jane's crew, we found enough money to keep us going for a while longer. Each couple made a point of winning over the locals, and when one of the waitresses asked us if we knew the "strange" Yanks who lived in the cabin at the edge of town, we told them that we had gone to meet them, only to find the place empty.

"They must have moved on," I told her. "There was no sign of them at all."

She breathed a sigh of relief, and I knew that the information would soon be flying throughout the city. The group in the cabin had made people nervous. On the contrary, we were quickly endearing ourselves to the locals.

"I don't know about anyone else," said Hanna, "but I'm finding it quite pleasant here. The people are nice and very accepting of us."

"We're a novelty," I said. "But that's not a bad thing. And they don't connect us in any way with the other group of Yanks. Natalie and I are feeling the same way. As we walk around the city, we see many positive things. People seem to take pride in

Perth. It's modern for the times. We know from the book Natalie bought that the gold rush is ending. That could be a good thing, giving the city time to grow on its own."

"I looked at the new Portal Finder," said Hanna. "Things aren't much different than they were before. It shows a few more incoming portals, including the one Jane and her friends used to get here, but there are no outgoing portals from Australia right now. There are more portals—incoming and outgoing—in places like China, Africa, and South America, but none are particularly inviting."

"How about America?" asked Hal.

"Some," answered Hanna. She looked at Natalie and me. "Believe it or not, your Hollow Rock portal is still there, in case you want to go back."

"That's okay, thanks," said Natalie with a laugh.

"So, if I'm hearing you right," said Simone, "unless we want to go traipsing across the globe in search of a better place, we are better off staying here."

It was nice to hear Simone be a part of the conversation. She had been so damaged by her eight years in the asylum she often chose just to listen and rarely contributed to discussions. According to Hal, though, Simone was more involved when it was just the two of them. He felt that, over time, she would begin to heal.

"I guess that's kind of what I'm saying," replied Hanna. "Alex and I have talked and have decided that we'd like to stay here for a while. There's something about the time and place that appeals to us."

"I think Natalie and I agree with that," I said. "We've talked about it, too. Our time in England was very comfortable, but the world we had left was going to barge in. We didn't want that. It's different here. The time is unfamiliar to all of us, as is the place."

"Simone and I have talked as well, and we agree," said Hal.

"Australia is a fascinating continent. If we travel, I think we'd like to see more of it. For the time being, though, I think we want to sit tight."

"I need time," said Simone.

"Well," I said, "I was going to say that anyone who wanted to keep on traveling could, and I would understand it, but I think the six of us agree."

"We still have to be on the alert for more eliminators," said Hanna. "We can't let our guard down."

"From all the eliminators we've killed," I said, "we have enough weapons for all of us. It's a step up from my Glock."

"We'll have to find jobs," said Alex, "but I think we all have skills that we can bring to the table."

"And the people here seem to like us," added Natalie.

I looked around the table. I was with friends, and we were all happy. That meant a lot. Could Natalie and I stay here for the rest of our lives?

Only time would tell.

The End

ABOUT THE AUTHOR

Andrew Cunningham is the author of the award-winning Amazon bestselling thriller **Wisdom Spring;** the terrorist/disaster thriller **Deadly Shore**; the *"Lies" Mystery Series*: **All Lies, Fatal Lies, Vegas Lies, Secrets & Lies, Blood Lies,** and **Buried Lies;** the post-apocalyptic *Eden Rising Series*: **Eden Rising, Eden Lost, Eden's Legacy** and **Eden's Survival;** and the *Yestertime Time Travel Series:* **Yestertime** and **The Yestertime Effect.** As A.R. Cunningham, he has written a series of five children's mysteries in the *Arthur MacArthur* series. Born in England, Andrew was a long-time resident of Cape Cod. He and his wife now live in Florida. Please visit his website at *arcnovels.com*, or his Facebook page, *Author Andrew Cunningham.*

Made in the USA
Monee, IL
18 May 2022

96636879R00134